Don't Panic.
Keep Breathing.
~

By Sarah Delany

Graphic Design (Cover) - Michael Pati Fuiava

Editing and Proofreading - Rebecca Andrews

Dedication

To my beloved sister Rachel Ayers,

whose best advice given to me was to, "Try before you buy."

I can picture you perfectly, with your hand covering your mouth, your face turning red, silent laughter about to come alive when you gasp the words, 'Sarah, you can't say that.' Well Rae I just did. Hope you are giggling in heaven.

I wish you were here to see this because out of everyone, you would have got a kick out of me becoming an author the most.

Born with a hole in your heart but left this Earth, leaving an even bigger one in ours.

Loving and missing you today, tomorrow and always.

Your little sister, Ser.

Contents

Prologue

I can't do this anymore.

I'm tired of being strong.

So tired.

I need these voices to stop.

I can't think of any other way out.

It will all be over soon.

I'll be free.

Everyone will be better off without me.

My demons have their clutches in me and some days I struggle to fend them off.

I can't go on this way.

I need it all to stop.

I'm sick of pretending I'm fine when I'm not.

How much longer can I hold the mask in place? I can feel it slipping.

I'm completely consumed with nowhere to turn.

I need help.

I don't want to burden anyone with my problems.

I've dealt with them this long.

What's a little while longer going to do?

I can do this.

I can keep fighting.

I'm strong.

But....

What happens when I have no fight left?

What becomes of me then?

Chapter 1

-- Tate --

"What the fuck bro?" JP screams at me, while I sit there trying hard to keep my emotions at bay. She's gone now. I made sure of that. I needed her to go. I saw it in her pained eyes. She knows she can't reach me. Her words cut me but I held it together long enough to get her away from me. Now I don't have to worry about feeling the pain anymore. I will push it down and bury it deep within me, never letting it escape.

"Are you listening to me?" he yells. I'm trying to block JP out. I wish he would leave too. Leave me to my void where I can contain everything. "You told me to leave her alone and look at what you did? You fucken broke her. She only wanted to be there for you. And I thought she was the cold one." It's funny how JP is on her side now instead of mine. I can't be on her side. She would crack me open and tear me apart. I can't have that, I wouldn't survive it.

"Look after her for me, please?" I ask him, before I push all my feelings for her away. His anger filled eyes stare back at me. I can see it written clearly on his face. He wants nothing better than to throat punch me. I don't blame him, I probably deserve it. I think the death of my sister is the only thing stopping him.

"I know you've had the shittiest day today bro but go fuck yourself," he hisses, before he turns his back on me. Great, now my own cousin hates me.

"John, come back here," his mum calls out to him. I'm so spaced out, I forgot they were in the room.

"Let him go," I tell her. I don't want to deal with JP's anger. I don't have the energy for anything except holding myself together. My aunt and uncle have a private conversation with their eyes. How they understand each other, I'll never know. My uncle leaves the room without saying a word and she moves to sit on the bed beside me.

"Tate, I know you're hurting but John and Tamsyn only want to be there for you. You could try letting them in instead of pushing them away. They both looked extremely hurt when you said you wouldn't come back," she says, sounding exactly like my mother. They are sisters after all. "I think you need to apologise to Tamsyn too. She came here to help and you acted like you could care less." I blankly stare at her. Her blonde hair and green eyes are the same as my mum's, which means they are too much like Quinn's. It's like seeing an older version of Quinn and my heart can't take it. It's a version of Quinn I will never get to see. She took that away from me. For a second my heart cracks, and a single tear from each eye escapes, rolling down my cheeks.

"Awww Tate, come here," she says, as she wraps her thin arms around me. I don't fight it. For this small moment, I flick the switch off and release the pain. I mourn for my twin; my better half. I wish it was her holding me in her arms instead. Knowing I will never hold her in my arms again makes the tears flow faster. I want her back. I want them both back. Quinn. Tamsyn. One I can't have, the other I don't deserve. I had to do it. I had to send her away. I can only hope that one day she will understand why I did it. My aunt must read my mind because she says, "It's not too late Tate, you could talk to her and explain. She would understand."

"I can't," I cry. I don't want to explain. I don't want to make things right. This is how it needs to be right now. So with a deep breath in, I exhale and flick the switch back on, letting go of the pain, letting go of Tamsyn and pushing the hurt away. I cage it up and throw away the key, hoping it won't get released again.

I disengage from my aunt and I see the look on her face. She knows the moment is over. She stands up and leaves because she knows I won't listen to anything she has to say now. I lie back on my bed and stare up at the ceiling, escaping everything by letting it float away. Her words play on repeat in my mind, 'Remember to shine'. She used my own words against me. Shining is the last thing I want to do. Don't think. Don't think. Don't think. The darkness takes over my mind and I let it because darkness blocks out the pain. Darkness is my new friend. I only wish someone was here to tell me how dangerous the darkness can be.

-- Tamsyn --

Out of breath, I slow my strides needing to calm down and I can't do that while running. I bend over, gasping for air while crying uncontrollably. It's not a pretty sight. It's dark out, I don't know the time. I left the house in such a rush, I didn't look at the clock. Being out here in the dark, alone and sober, creeps me out so I start speed walking in the direction of home. I can't be too far away. When I finally get my breathing under control, I hear a 'BEEP BEEP BEEP' and it's getting louder. I spin around as the familiar car pulls up beside me.

The window winds down and I hear JP softly say, "Jump in Tamsyn, I'll give you a ride home." I don't have the energy to argue so I do as he's asked. Opening the passenger door and sliding in, I keep my eyes directed out the front window not wanting to make eye contact with him. "I'm sorry," he quietly says, and the pull to look at him has my eyes glancing his way.

"You've got nothing to apologise for. It wasn't your fault." I let out a sigh. "Maybe I should have listened to you in the first place. You did try to warn me away from him, remember? Guess you didn't think it would end like this, " I say, as the tears well up again.

"Don't pay attention to Tate. He just lost his sister and doesn't know what he's doing. He truly cares about you," he says, trying to convince me but it doesn't work. I saw it in Tate's eyes. I heard it in his voice. I'm not what he needs. I can't heal him of his pain.

"It's fine JP. It's better this way. I know what he's going through. I'm causing him more pain by being near him and it's the last thing I want to do. Sometimes it is better to take a step back and let things be, no matter how badly you want or need to help. I have to accept that," I tell him, as he pulls up outside my house and puts the car into park.

"You gonna be alright?" he asks, angling his body towards me.

"I was coping fine before he came along. I'll learn to cope after he's gone," I say, dropping my gaze to my lap. I don't admit it to JP but I wasn't coping at all before Tate. Just breathe Tam. Breathe. "Are you going to the funeral?" I ask, as I steady my breathing.

"Yeah, we will probably fly down in a few days when they know more about the funeral arrangements. I didn't know he wasn't planning on coming back." I had gathered as much by the look of shock plastered on his face after Tate's big announcement.

"Well now we know," I say, as I open the door and step back out into the night.

"Bye, Tamsyn," I hear him say, as I drag myself up the path, not wanting to go home but having nowhere else to go.

Grasping the handle, I twist it open and enter the quiet house. I don't want to wake Mum if I can avoid it so I tiptoe across the wooden floor and up the stairs. Safely in my room, I climb under my blankets and release the hurt I've been holding in. Muffling my cries with my pillow, I press it harder against my face the more I let loose. With my irreparable heart breaking, I cry until I'm drained. Letting go of the boy who was helping fix me. The boy who won't let me return the favour and do the same for him.

The next morning I find dragging myself out of bed is tiring in itself. I tossed and turned all night, thoughts of Tate keeping me awake. I would rather stay in bed all day than go to school but I don't want to have to explain anything to Mum. With the decision made, I push myself up and out of bed, forcing myself to go to the bathroom and begin my morning routine. Scott and Rafe are due to arrive soon so we can walk to school. I wonder if JP told them what happened. Did he only want to fix me because he couldn't fix Quinn? Is that what I was to him? A pity project? How dumb was I to think anyone could like me. I'm such a mess. I'm better off alone. Oh my gosh, are the guys only my friends because of Tate? Where does that leave me now? Will they not want to be around me either? No, it can't have been one sided. He does care about me. I'm sure of it. Dressed in my uniform and ready to leave for school, I sit on my bed, barely keeping myself together. My thoughts run rampant.

"Tamsyn, the boys are here," I hear my mum call. I'm about to leave my room when I remember I haven't put Tate's star in my pocket. I glance at my bedside table where it is hidden in the top drawer. My fingers itch to locate it and place it in my pocket but my brain won't let me. Sadly, I turn and walk away, forcing myself to leave my room and the star behind. The star that had become my lifeline; a star shining in a sea of darkness, showing me the way like the north star guiding lost travellers. There's only darkness now, with no light in sight. I can feel myself slipping into the shadows and this time, I don't know if I have the strength to pull myself out. I needed Tate's help before. He was helping me to break the surface from which I was drowning. How will I do this on my own? I have to try.

"Tamsyn, you coming bub?" my mum calls louder. She must think I didn't hear her the first time. Taking a deep breath, I fall back into old habits and plaster on the fake smile I haven't needed in a while and skip down the stairs to the guys.

"Hey guys," I say, with fake cheeriness. They stare at me from the bottom of the stairs with furrowed brows. It looks like JP filled them in and they don't understand why I'm so happy.

"Hi T," Scott says, as I reach them.

"Let's get going, shall we? We don't want to be late." I don't want them starting a conversation with my mum so I herd them towards the front door, wanting to get out of the house at record speed. "Bye Mum," I call over my shoulder, as I push past the guys and hope they will follow me out the door, which they do, after saying goodbye to my mum.

As we fall into line, walking to school, no one says anything and an awkward silence hangs over us. Please don't let them bring it up. That would be great. But no, I spoke too soon. I'm not that lucky.

"So T, JP filled us in about what happened with Tate," Scott says. I sigh and turn to them with unshed tears in my eyes. I thought I'd be able to hold it in longer.

"Awww Tamsyn, it's okay girl," Rafe says, as he folds me into his arms, making the tears tip over and escape. "Honestly, ignore whatever he said. He's not in the right headspace. He didn't mean it. He is crazy about you," he says, trying to comfort me, but it doesn't work. The pain was inflicted and it hurts thinking about it.

"And if you, for one second, doubt how we feel about you, please don't. We care about you as much as Tate does. We aren't going anywhere. You can't get rid of us that easily," Scott tells me. I unwrap myself from Rafe's embrace and wipe my eyes, pulling myself together again.

"Thanks guys. It means a lot," I tell them, meaning it from the bottom of my broken heart. I don't know what I would do without them in my life. I've come to care about these guys and I can't stand the thought of them leaving too. Losing their friendship would sting. We continue walking while the pair of them start cracking jokes. I laugh at the right times and join in when I can but old habits are hard to break. I can feel myself falling back into self destructive patterns. Without Tate's keen observation skills, who will notice I'm drowning again, unable to breach the surface of the waves crashing down around me? I can only hope I get thrown a life raft.

The day passes in a blur. I don't pay attention in my classes, finding it too hard to concentrate. At lunchtime I grab a sandwich, my lack of appetite returning, not that it was fully back in the first place. I noticed the absence of JP at school today. I'm guessing we won't see him until after the funeral. I wonder if Tate has left yet. I push thoughts of Tate aside. Him being gone is like being stabbed in the heart with a hot poker repeatedly, over and over; the pain too unbearable. If I can hold on until tonight when I'm in my room alone, I can let myself break apart in peace, without anyone to witness how utterly broken I am.

The guys walk me home after school in what will be our new normal for a while. That is, until JP comes back to school. Entering the house, I plaster on the smile I need to get past my mum.

"Have you heard from Tate, bub?" she asks, and the sound of his name is like a whip across my body; sharp and painful.

"No Mum, I haven't. He was heading back home today for the funeral. I'm not sure when he will be back," I tell her, acting as though everything is fine between me and him.

"Try not to worry about him, Tammy. He'll get through this," she says, as I take off up the stairs, needing to get away from her. I escape to my room, climb under the blankets and let the pain out. As I break, I wish the boy who doesn't want my help was here to comfort me. In his arms, I find solace and the only peace I have known since my dad's passing. His arms feel like home whenever he wraps them around me and now, without them, I feel homeless. Thinking about my dad brings on another wave of tears. This grief feels neverending, knocking me back down again when I least expect it.

-- Tate --

I'm on the plane heading home. Home, it's such a funny word to me now. I don't know where my home is anymore. I didn't want to leave in the first place, I was forced to and now, I don't want to return. Not without Quinn there. How can she be gone?

JP couldn't look at me when I said goodbye. He's become a brother to me in the short while I stayed with him. It pains me I have to leave him but I won't admit it to his face. Tamsyn. I can't think about her. Thoughts of her are firmly locked away in a fireproof vault, keeping me safe.

I lose myself staring out the airplane window, watching the white fluffy clouds pass by and the sea of blue sky stretching out further than I can see. I wonder if Quinn is out there somewhere, living on the breeze, dancing from one cloud to the next. Before I know it, we are preparing to land then we are bumping along the runway. I drag my feet through the airport and when my mum catches sight of me, I see her fall apart. The tears freely flow down her face as she clings to me. My dad looks at me over her shoulder as I unconsciously hug her back. He looks older now, as if the trauma from Quinn's situation has aged him greatly, in just a few short months. A couple of months, is that all I've been gone? It feels longer, like a whole lifetime has passed. It feels as though I've known Tamsyn forever. Funny how time works. My eyes stay dry. The numbness has completely set in now, keeping all of my emotions in check. I can't let them leak out because then I will shatter and I can't have that when I've only managed to get the duct tape to stick again. Numb is good. It'll help me survive this. I don't know any other way.

The drive home is filled with a mixture of small talk and silence, none of us knowing what to say. If I talk and tell them how I'm feeling then I'll explode, so I choose silence and contain my feelings. I don't want to burden them with the craziness rattling around in my head. It's easier if I keep it to myself. I can deal with it. I have this numbness feeling down pat. I'll keep to the darkness, not feeling it but feeding it all my emotions. Rage, sadness, unbearable grief, guilt and the list goes on. All the emotions fuel the darkness, slowly swallowing me whole.

When my dad drives up the rocky driveway to my house, I have to take a breath to steady myself. Don't think Tate. Don't do it. I release my breath and along with it, the emotions. I feel a sense of stillness settle into my very bones. This is exactly what I need. I exit the car and follow my parents through the big red door. I always hated that door. When we painted the house a few years ago, Quinn insisted the door had to be red. She didn't care about the colour of the house but said the door had to be bright red. Then we could say things like, 'Ours is the house with the big red door,' she would justify. She was quirky like that, always wanting to stand out in some odd way. Perhaps it is a twin thing, wanting to separate yourself from your twin by being oddly unique. I don't know. I never asked her why she wanted the door red and being the selfish prick I was, I wouldn't have cared what her answer was.

Somehow I made it to my room and I'm lying down on my old bed. Losing myself in my head has my body operating on flight mode. I get from point A to point B without registering what's happening. My posters of basketball players are still on the wall. It's like I never left and nothing's changed. But everything has changed. My whole world has crumbled like a wet cookie dunked in milk and it can't be put back together.

My parents let me be. They don't bother checking in on me. I stay lying on my bed while the sun sets and dusk seeps in. I don't get up to eat. I'll eat later. I know sleep won't come. It was hard enough to sleep before, when Quinn was in a coma. Now she's gone, all I can do is stare into the darkness surrounding me and hope exhaustion takes over and drags me into a deep slumber. A boy is allowed to hope but I don't like my chances.

Chapter 2

-- Tate --

Sitting cross legged on the cold grass, my only thought is to get this done. I need to do this for her. I put the finishing touches on my small gift and carefully take it inside to the bathroom, treating it with the utmost care. Something I wish I had done with Quinn. I look at myself in the mirror. My black long sleeved dress shirt is neatly ironed with my matching black trousers. Black shiny shoes complete my outfit. I've decided I hate black. It signifies death to me now. Death and pain. I put some effort in and gel my blond hair back. It could do with a cut. It's too long on the sides for my liking. I don't know this person staring back at me, a stranger's reflection is all I see. I'm having an out of body experience. My soul exists out of this body and this shell of a person carries me around but there is no emotional connection between the two parts. Taking a deep inhale, I place my gift carefully in my pocket so as not to ruin it and exit the bathroom. I'm leaving to go do the hardest thing I have ever had to endure, something I wouldn't wish on my worst enemy. I'm going to bury my sister.

JP and his parents arrived two days ago and we've hardly said a word to each other. He's tried but I can tell he's still angry over how I treated Tamsyn and the fact I won't return with him. I can't. I'm safer here where I can hide. I have to stop myself from asking how she is or if he's seen her. I have no right to that information. She's better off without me.

People have been coming in and out of the house since I got back. Old friends have come around to pay their respects and family members have popped in, trying to console Mum and Dad. 'Terrible tragedy,' they say or 'Gone too soon'. My new favourite is when they say 'She's at peace now'. It's my favourite because every time I hear it, I picture myself throat punching whoever says it. How the hell would you know if she's at peace, Karen? People spew the same sentimental garbage at you, recycling what they have heard before. Those words don't help. They are better off keeping their big traps shut and not saying anything. Nothing can make this better so they can take their band aid words away and shove it.

The rage inside bubbles to the surface every so often but I manage to taper it back down. Sometimes it sneaks up on me with no warning, especially if someone says anything remotely annoying which has my brain listing all the reasons why their comment pissed me off in the first place.

I look up at the funeral home. She's not having her funeral in a church because my mum doesn't think it's right. I haven't seen my mum without tears since I arrived. My dad is doing his best holding it together, trying to be an anchor for Mum. He has to hold her up, she looks on the verge of fainting with the horrible task we have ahead of us. I've told myself if I can keep myself together today, I can break down for a minute tonight when I'm alone. But not now. For now, I need to be numb and hollow to get through this horrible day.

It's the worst day of my life so far which makes it one of the days I'd most like to forget. Brains are tricky things however and my brain has a mind of its own. It has made this day more memorable, more vivid and can recall every detail in precision. They say as you grow older you forget moments and what you are remembering is a memory of that moment.

I know for a fact that this day and all its moments will forever be etched into my very soul.

Her dark cherry coffin shines as it sits stationed at the front of the quiet room. The only input I had for her funeral was to have a closed casket. I couldn't handle the thought of an open coffin. I don't want to remember her like that. Lifeless. I want to hold the memory of her laughing and smiling in my mind. My parents tried to convince me to go visit her at a viewing, when she was set up in the coffin before today, but I couldn't do it. I couldn't face her. They chose to go and returned looking more distraught than they did before they left. I think I dodged a bullet.

Dad slowly approaches the microphone to start his eulogy. Don't think. Don't think. Don't think. I turn my numbness factor up a notch, trying to zone out because any stories he has to share will break me. I don't want to remember happy memories when she's in a coffin, not two metres from me. Dead and lifeless. I stare at my shiny shoes and watch the drips of water hit them. I wipe my eyes, try to draw a breath into my lungs and focus on my inhale.

I raise my head with tear soaked eyes and look at the shattered face of my dad. He stammers over his words, trying to stay strong as he delivers his speech. Every so often, he needs to stop and gather himself. I can see him visibly take a breath to pull himself back together so he can carry on. It's not fair. Why did this have to happen to my family? We shouldn't be here. Not like this. How could Quinn do this to us? To me?

Other family members take their turns, recalling fond memories they have of Quinn. Most of them include me as we were inseparable at one stage in life, making it that much harder to listen. It didn't help that we were twins and always wanted to do everything together until I got older. I thought I was too cool to hang out with my sister and wanted my own life. My own friends. I was too busy with my new life to realise Quinn was struggling with the distance I put between us. Struggling with a darkness that has now become my closest companion.

It's time for the pall bearers to grab the handles so I rise from my seat and walk over to her coffin. I glance at the framed photo on top, it's of her beautiful smiling face; my Quinny. I bend down delivering a kiss to her shiny coffin, pretending it's her forehead and I'm tucking her into bed like I did when we were younger. Mum grasps the framed picture of Quinn and clutches it tightly, close to her chest. With eyes full of unshed tears, my hands shake as I take the cold bar in my grip. Dad takes the opposite side to me. JP and his dad take another two spots and then my cousin Pete and his dad take up the remaining spaces. And we lift. Walking slowly with the melancholy music serenading us, we carry my darling sister out of the funeral home and place her in the hearse. As everyone exits the building, I watch as my sister gets driven away, heading to her final resting place.

The sun is shining but I don't feel it's heat. I don't feel anything. Quinn gets lowered into the ground and everyone throws in their red rose petals and shovels in their handfuls of dirt. I take a few steps forward and retrieve my gift from my pocket, the daisy chain crown I'd made earlier. Quinn was always bugging me to make these damn things with her. That's the only reason I know how to make one. I stretch it out into a circle and gently drop it into the grave and watch while it floats down to her coffin. My little flower queen. I quietly stand there, looking down into her grave as the hole fills up. Saying my final goodbye silently, I turn and walk away. My broken heart is trying to keep the duct tape intact but it's bursting at the seams. If I don't hold on for dear life, I know I will lose the struggle and my heart will rip apart more than humanly possible.

I don't notice JP has followed me until we are beside the car, waiting for everyone else to finish up at her grave. I couldn't stand there another second or I would have broken. I swallow the lump of emotion in my throat, forcing it down. The wake is at our house. I'm hoping I will be able to escape to my room, away from everyone. I want to be alone. No one can comfort me. They only say the wrong thing. JP stands there silently. I wonder how long the silence will last this time, before he cracks. Everyone finally disperses from the grave. I hop in the car and keep my eyes down, not wanting to give in to the pull of her grave. I can't look back as I leave. I can't think about her being left there, alone in the cold ground with no one to protect her, so I numb myself more and drift further into the dark.

The mood in the house is somber. Strangers approach me and offer their commiserations. Old friends from school tell me, 'They're sorry,' or they don't know what to say so they give me an awkward hug instead. It's been months since I saw these people last. My mates Pierce and Xander are here too. I haven't heard much from them since I left to go to JP's. After Quinn went into her coma, they visited me in the hospital once but they stopped coming around. Xander always had a sweet spot for Quinn and I think it hurt him more than he'd admit to see her like that. I stare at my curly haired friend now and can see the devastation on his face. It's hard to remember I'm not the only one in pain.

"Tate, you want to go somewhere?" Pierce asks, as he opens his jacket to show me the full bottle of whiskey he has hidden there. I nod in agreement and walk to my room as JP, Pierce and Xander follow. We all find a spot in my room. JP sits at my desk, I sit on my bed with Pierce sitting on the opposite end while Xander sits on the floor. Pierce twists the cap off the bottle and holds it up saying, "To Quinn," as he takes a swig and passes it to me. Holding the glass bottle in my hand, I fling my head back as I gulp it down, hissing out a breath as the burn travels down my throat, warming my belly. This is what I need to drown my thoughts completely. We pass the bottle around as JP puts on Spotify to play softly in the background. The bottle is a third of the way through when JP breaks the silence.

"How's school going for you guys?" he says, directing the question to my friends. He knows I don't want to talk right now. It works for me.

"Good," they both reply in unison. The alcohol does its job, numbing me further so I close my eyes, breathe and wait for the darkness to drown me.

"Give me your number bro?" JP says to one of them, and I hear Pierce reciting his digits for him to save.

Time is lost on me. We could have been in my room for minutes or it could be hours, I don't know. The half empty bottle has loosened the guys' lips and they're laughing, telling stories to each other. Stories about people the others don't know and stories they all have of me as I'm the common denominator in this situation. I sit there quietly and listen, distracting myself by getting lost in their talk. JP's phone pings signalling a text message so he retrieves it from his pocket. I watch as he tries to hide the obvious glance my way. Now I know it's someone wanting to know about me.

I don't care who it is until he says, "It's Tamsyn, wanting to make sure you're okay." I wince hearing her name.

"Oooh, who's Tamsyn?" Xander innocently asks.

"Nobody," I deadpan, as JP shakes his head.

"Bro..," he starts.

"Leave it," I angrily say, as I snatch the bottle from Pierce and quickly leave the room. I stumble through the groups of people situated all over the house and escape out the back door, heading nowhere in particular. I need to get away. But how can you escape the biggest problem when the problem is you?

I have no recollection of where I ended up, only knowing I polished the bottle off. My last memory was of Tamsyn's devastated face, the last time I saw her and the photo of Quinn smiling, on top of her casket, as they merged into one.

Chapter 3

-- Tamsyn --

I couldn't help myself. Knowing the funeral was today, I had to check in with JP and see how Tate was doing. His reply was, 'He's as good as can be expected,' whatever that means. I had to force myself not to text back and ask him to elaborate. JP was with him and I knew he would look after him. I need to get out of the house. It has been a week since Tate left and I'm over crying myself to sleep every night. I'm getting little sleep, if any. I need to get out of my head.

I want to feel numb, and after the vague reply from JP, I want to forget everything. I have on my baggy track pants and grab a jumper and zip it up, flipping the hood over my head. I slip on my sneakers and quietly creep down the stairs, trying not to disturb my mum in her room. Once I'm in the living room, I grab the first bottle out of the cabinet and tiptoe to the front door, quietly letting myself out. Cold air blows around me so I wrap my arms around my waist. Once I'm clear of my house, I unscrew the lid and tip my head back. The brown liquor scorches my throat on its way down. I cough after I swallow, not enjoying it. It's not for enjoyment so it doesn't matter. I suffer through the burning sensation. It's a small price to pay for the prize I will receive in return. Numbness.

I take a few more gulps of it as I head in the familiar direction. My feet are taking me where I need to go. As I approach the old wooden dock, I glance at my surroundings. It's peaceful out here with only the chirping of insects to keep me company. No one else is around and I can pretend it's just me. Me and my dock. I take a seat right on the edge, letting my feet dangle over the side. I look down into the dark calm water. It looks like it would be quiet down there. I take another mouthful of the awful tasting liquor, deciding never to drink bourbon again after tonight. Vodka is the way to go. A buzz has started to kick in but I long for the numb feeling I know will follow. I can practically hear my mum chiding me, 'Patience is a virtue, Tamsyn.'

My phone buzzes and I check the caller ID, it's JP. I don't want to hear about Tate right now so I ignore it, sending it to voicemail. Persistent guy rings again and I decline, not caring if he knows I'm blatantly ignoring him. A text comes through not long after.

JP: Tamsyn pls let me know you are ok.

Tamsyn: I'm fin3 leabe me alone.

He doesn't reply so I put my phone down and take a big skull needing to forget everything, if only for a night. It's not long before my phone is ringing again. I'm so annoyed at JP for bugging me, I answer without checking the caller ID.

"JP, quit it already. I said leave me alone," I angrily yell into the phone.

"Tamsyn, where are you Petal?"

"Rafe?" I ask, and pull my phone away from my ear to check whose name is on the screen. And sure enough, it's Rafe's.

"Please Petal, tell me where you are so JP can stop worrying."

I let out a sigh and say, "I'm at the dock."

"Are you okay?" he asks.

"Yeah, I'm fine. I just needed to get out of the house," I tell him, trying not to slur my words so he doesn't catch on to the fact I've been drinking.

"Okay, be careful," he says, and quickly hangs up. I stare at the phone, thinking it was easier than I thought to convince him I'm fine. Ten minutes later and a sweaty, puffing Rafe is dumping himself next to me, having run all the way here. He eyes up the bourbon bottle but doesn't say a word as I continue to skull mouthfuls down. I offer him a drink but he declines.

I lean my head on his shoulder and the more numb my mind becomes, the less control I have over my emotions. The tears fall freely down my face. Rafe doesn't say a word the entire time he's with me. He only puts an arm around my shoulder, holding me tightly, while I let all the pain out before I drift into darkness.

I wake up in my bed in the morning, remembering Rafe but there's no sign of him. He must have carried me home and snuck me into my bed, without my mum noticing. My head is killing me so I sit up in bed when I notice the note on my bedside table. It's from Rafe. 'These will help,' is all he's written. I find a couple of paracetamol and a bottle of water next to the note. I wash them down and have to stop myself from vomiting. The alcohol I wanted so badly last night, threatening to resurface. I grab my waste basket just in case.

I move to my door and yell out, "Mum, I'm not feeling well. I'm going to stay in bed."

"Oh no. Do you need anything, bub?" she asks, in her concerned tone.

"No, it's okay. I took some pain relief. I'll hopefully be able to sleep it off," I tell her, hoping my hangover will lessen after a nap.

"Okay sweetie, rest up," she says, unaware her daughter was drinking last night. I hop back into bed and find my phone on the bedside table. I grab it and quickly send a text.

Tamsyn: Thanks for last night.

Instantly a reply comes through.

Rafe: Don't mention it :)

Putting my phone on silent, I snuggle under the covers, pulling them up to my chin and stare at the ceiling until I drift off to sleep.

-- Tate --

Ugh, why is it so sunny in my room? I cover my eyes from the brightness. Those birds sound awfully close. I slowly peel my eyes open and view my surroundings. Chill seeps into my bones as I realise I've fallen asleep on the grass. I push myself up from the ground and feel the dewy green blades under my hands. With a foggy head I glance around, not sure where I am. I sit there for a minute, trying to get my bearings. Bending my knees, I place my arms across them and lower my head, still feeling drunk and try to calm the spinning in my head. I think back to the day before. Quinn's funeral. Tamsyn texted JP. Me leaving the house and wandering around. I raise my head again and take another look around. There's a few white buildings in the distance with forest green roofs. They look familiar. Dammit, I'm at my old school. I fell asleep on the football field. Great. This is one of the last places I want to be. This school holds too many memories of Quinn.

I pat my pockets to locate my phone and pull it out. That's when I notice the not so discrete pile of vomit next to me. My new thing seems to be sleeping outside and vomiting my guts out. Just great. The time on my phone says it's seven thirty. At least it's a Saturday so nobody should be around. I heave myself up to stand, swaying while I do. I had way too much to drink last night. I shake my head to try and rid it of the fogginess. My eye catches the empty bottle, lying a few feet away from me. I walk over and pick it up and stumble across the field towards the school buildings, with the glass bottle dangling from my fingers. I dump the empty bottle in a trash can and keep up my slow stagger as I walk towards the entrance of the school. I don't want to go through the school but it's the fastest route to get home so I focus on the end goal and nothing else. My head is too vulnerable at the moment and more susceptible to a flood of memories, centred around Quinn, so I focus on putting one foot in front of the other.

I check my phone again and see I have a barrage of missed texts and calls. I open them up. Three missed calls from JP, one from my dad and three texts from JP.

JP: Come home bro, I'm sorry I shouldn't have mentioned her.

JP: I'm starting to get worried, it's been hours now, can you come home please?

JP: Your dad came looking for you and he figured out you had taken off so now he's worried too. Please let me know you're alright.

His last text came in at midnight. I could care less if they were worried. They were lucky I made it to the funeral. I was close to not turning up. I can't deal with people at the moment. I'm better off by myself. They either remind me of Quinn or remind me of Tamsyn and I don't want to think about either of them. Saying their names in my head tears a strip off my heart.

I stagger through the concrete gate and turn in the direction of home. My head is killing me with a constant throbbing behind the eyes. I like the fact alcohol sends me into a forgotten darkness but I could do without the hangovers. Getting myself home takes longer than I remember. It could do with the fact the alcohol is still very much swimming in my veins. With the amount I drank yesterday to black out, I'm not surprised I'm still a tad drunk. As I reach my house, I stop and look up at it, shielding my eyes from the bright sun with my hand. Our off white house stands there, and for some reason looks smaller than I remember. It's because Quinn's presence is missing from it. I drag my feet up to the big bright red door and twist the handle, hoping it opens. Luckily it does and I creep inside, silently closing it behind me. I try to get to my room before I'm seen but my dad is sitting at the kitchen table. His tired eyes look at me and I know he's been waiting up all night.

"Tate?" he softly calls, and I don't want to make matters worse so I take a seat opposite him. "Do you want to talk about it?" he asks me, as I look down at the table. I shake my head. How can talking with him help, he's got his own grief to worry about. I don't want to burden him with my pain when he already has Mum to look after, she's struggling too. We all are. I don't want to see his face, because I don't want to see the anguish behind his eyes I know is lurking there. He lets out a deep sorrow filled sigh and says, "If you ever change your mind and want to talk, I'm here son. Remember that."

Without looking at him, I push my chair back and stand up. I walk over to the sink, fill a glass with cold water and gulp it down, hoping it will help with the banging in my head. I refill it again and take a few more sips before I rinse it and leave it in the sink. Walking to my room, I open the door and find it empty. For a second, I wonder what happened to the guys before I shove that thought aside. It doesn't matter. All that matters right now, is sleep.

I kick off my shoes, and unzip my pants pulling them down and throwing them in the corner of my room. My shirt follows. I might burn those clothes. I never want to wear them again. They only serve as a reminder of the worst day of my life. I pull the covers back and crawl into bed. With the alcohol still in my system and the exhaustion from this week's events, sleep comes surprisingly easy and I sail away into what I hope will last forever.

I throw myself into a sitting position. Panting, I throw the drenched covers off as I'm covered in sweat. I inhale deeper and slow my breathing down. It wasn't real. It was only a dream, I tell myself. It was remarkably vivid, it had me believing it was real. I was running when I came upon the dock, where I found Tamsyn that night. I had slowed my steps and saw a hand reaching up from the water. I'd dropped to the ground, lying down and reaching my hand out, trying to reach them. Their head had surfaced and it was Tamsyn then she'd sunk again. When she resurfaced, it was Quinn's face instead. I started panicking, trying to reach her but she had sunk too. I had grasped the hand and pulled them up but it wasn't either of them. It was my own face staring back at me. I'd been in such a state of shock, I'd dropped my hand and I had sunk, my hand disappearing into the dark water. That's when I woke up.

I run my hands down my face, wiping the moisture away. Getting out of bed, I stare at the sweat covered sheets. I can't get to sleep lying on those. I strip all the sheets off my bed and throw them in the corner to join my discarded clothes. I glance at the alarm clock beside my bed and it's only been a couple hours. I climb back on my bed not caring that I'm lying on a bare mattress. I grab my headphones, plug them in and turn on my Spotify playlist. I hope the loud music will be a reprieve and drown out any thoughts trying to take root. I stare at the plain ceiling, numbing myself and waiting for exhaustion to kick in again.

I blink, as I slowly come out of my sleep and the clock comes into focus. It's one in the afternoon. At least I've managed to get some undisturbed sleep today. It's quiet. I notice my phone beside my head, my headphones having come free of my ears during sleep. I sit up and stretch my arms over my head. Leaning back against the wall, I hear a knocking at my door.

"Come in," I say through a yawn. JP enters with a tired look on his face. He looks like he just woke up.

"Hey bro," he says, as he comes in. He eyes up my bare bed and the discarded sheets in the corner then sits by my feet at the end of the bed. I don't say anything, knowing he will start talking in his own time. He runs a hand over his head and lets out a sigh.

"You okay?" he asks.

"Yeah, I'm fine," I say, trying to contain my anger. I'm sick of people asking me that question. Obviously I'm not fine, and asking me a dumb question like that irritates me more.

"Where did you end up last night?" he asks.

"Nowhere in particular. I got home this morning in one piece so there was no need to worry," I tell him. He looks at me and I see the pain in his eyes. He's worried about me but right now I want to be by myself.

"I do worry about you, it's hard not to. I know Quinn died but the way you're acting isn't you."

"Don't. Don't bring her up. I don't want to talk about her right now," I tell him sternly.

"What about Tamsyn then? Do you want to talk about her?" he says, raising his voice. Her name hits me in the gut. I wish he would stop bringing her up. I ignore him, hoping he will drop it. "She was drinking by herself last night. Rafe managed to find her at the dock, where she ended up crying herself to sleep. He carried her home and snuck her into the house so her mum wouldn't know." I wince inside and hope it doesn't show on my face. "The worst part was she kept going on about you. She was worried about you." I shake my head, this is not what I need to hear right now.

"I'm no good for her. I'm a mess at the moment. She's better off without me," I say, hoping it will convince him to let the subject of Tamsyn go.

"Why don't you at least come back to school with me and see how it goes?" he asks.

"Leave it JP. I told you, I'm not coming back. I should have never come in the first place," I say.

"She needs you bro." I release a sigh and press my fingers to my temples, feeling a headache coming on.

"Please, I can't do anything for her right now. I need my space to grieve for my sister so please, drop it already," I plead with him. He hangs his head as we sit in silence for a few minutes.

"Fine, but if you need me for anything, call me please. It doesn't matter what time of the day it is." I nod, and he exits the room knowing our conversation is over. It was over as soon as he mentioned Tamsyn. She's better off without me. I'm no good for her. She deserves better than me. I'm too broken right now. I would be a liar if I said I wasn't worried about her. She shouldn't be drinking like that. I wonder what made her start drinking like that again. No, I can't fall back into those patterns. I can't spend my time worrying about her anymore. I push thoughts of her aside and bury them deep down inside. I don't have the energy to worry about her, it would be far too overwhelming like a swimmer caught in a riptide, using all their strength swimming against the current, only to be hit by a huge wave with no means of escape.

Chapter 4

-- Tamsyn --

The week has passed in a blur. I couldn't focus on school work even if I wanted to. I don't have the energy to engage in any classes. I feel lost without Tate. He was the lifeline I needed to pull myself above the waves so I was treading water, but now I'm drowning in it again, not able to surface. I don't have the energy to keep pretending any more or plaster on my old reliable fake smile. The guys include me at school but it feels different without Tate here. JP arrived back a few days ago so he's been picking us all up for school and dropping us all home. I'm not sure whose idea it was for all of us to go to school together as it used to just be me, Tate and JP. Maybe JP didn't want to be alone with me. I don't know. I sometimes catch him looking at me with a sad expression on his face. I think he feels responsible for how Tate talked to me that night because he was the reason I was there. If I didn't go see Tate that night, I would be stuck in a worse limbo than I am now, not knowing what was happening between us. I probably wouldn't have received a goodbye. None of that is JP's fault, he couldn't know what was going to happen. Now they probably feel stuck with me because of him. They wouldn't have talked to me or given me the time of day if it wasn't for him. Now he's left me behind and they're here to pick up the pieces but the biggest piece to my puzzle is missing and I'm not sure how they can possibly fix me.

I hate human bio now. It went from being my favourite class to my most hated class in the space of a day. Every time I sit at my table, his missing presence is like a nail getting hammered through my heart. Scott and Rafe include me during class. I catch them both, giving his empty seat glances, when they think I'm not looking. I think they both miss him as well. In his current state of mind, Tate didn't think to say goodbye to them. JP didn't tell us much when he returned. He said the funeral was nice and Quinn would have liked it. He tried not to talk too much about Tate. I wanted to ask how he was doing but the voice in my head stopped me, this time. Telling me if he needed you, you would have heard from him. He probably wouldn't appreciate me begging for scraps of information about him from his cousin.

I've nearly taken the plunge and dialled his number a couple of times. I can never bring myself to follow through. A small piece of me still clings to him and hopes he will come back, telling me he didn't mean it, and he feels the same way I do. That he can heal with me, instead of without me. Will he ever come back for me or am I kidding myself? Is it dumb to hope for something he made clear wasn't going to happen? He could change his mind. I'm sure it was just his grief talking.

Here I sit in human bio, with my head lying on my arms, trying my damndest to keep it together. It's tiring. Ms. Chadwick is droning on about whatever topic it is we are learning about today. I haven't taken any notes since he left. Scott kindly has taken it upon himself to take notes and photocopy a set for me after each class. He gives them to me every day on the ride home from school. Without warning, the tears fall from my eyes and I can't keep them at bay. I have no other thought but to get out of the class before nosey eyes get drawn my way, looking for another piece of gossip to keep them entertained. I hastily push my chair back and rush from the room, only hearing Ms. Chadwick call my name when I've already left the class behind. I need the safety of my sanctuary. Luckily it's empty. That's the upside to leaving class in the middle of a lesson. There are less people about so there's less chance someone will see me. I lower the lid, climb up onto the toilet and hug myself close in the last cubicle. Breathe Tam breathe. It's only tears. Let them out and move on. I let my anguish out and sit with my misery for a few minutes. I miss Tate. Why wasn't I enough for him? Why couldn't I save us both? Will he come back for me? All these unanswered, neverending questions swamp my mind.

I sit cuddled in my little ball when the bell for the end of school rings. I should get up and grab my things from class but I need to pull myself together first. The thought of the guys waiting and worrying about me has me exiting the stall and stumbling over to the sink. I turn the cold tap on and splash handfuls of water on my face, trying to remove some of the blotchiness my tears have caused. The door opens and I avoid eye contact with whoever it is, focussing on the cold water instead.

"Hey Tamsyn, are you okay?" I hear quietly next to me. I look at the person through the mirror. I can see the pain clearly on my face and don't try to hide it.

"Yeah Penny, I'll be alright. Having one of those days," I say to the girl who has only ever been kind to me.

"Yeah, I know exactly what you mean," she says, as she pulls out some paper towels and hands them to me so I can dry my face.

"Thanks," I say in return, as I dab at my wet face.

"You doing anything tonight?" she asks.

"No, I was planning on hanging out at home. What about you?"

"I'm having another party. My parents are away again so I thought why not. You should come with the guys," she says. Her invitation sounds genuine. Ever since I found out Leyla and Chloe were backstabbing cows, I've avoided girls like the plague. It was easier hanging out with the guys. At least they are straight with each other. There's no deceit and lies between them, no games being played behind each others' backs.

What you see is what you get with them and I will forever be grateful for that.

"I'll ask them," I tell Penny, and a smile lights up her face. Perhaps she does want me to come and the invite wasn't because she pities me.

"Cool. Hopefully I'll see you there," she says as I exit the bathroom, throwing the paper towels in the bin. I hurry through the hallways and out into the carpark. Knowing Scott, he probably grabbed my things for me.

"There you are," I hear from my side, and turn to look up at Rafe's worried face.

"Sorry, I had a moment. I'm fine now," I tell him, as he throws his arm over my shoulders.

"We are here for you if you need us, Petal." I glance up at him and smile. All these boys are such sweethearts. I don't deserve it.

"Oh, I left my bag behind in class. Scott didn't manage to grab it, did he?" I ask, remembering my bag.

"As a matter of fact, he did. He packed all your books into it too," he cheerily says, like he's proud of Scott for grabbing my things. As we near the car, I see Scott and JP waiting outside on the hood instead of in their seats. Since we are together, I take it as the perfect opportunity to bring up the party. I hope the invite will distract them so they don't worry about why I was hanging out in the bathroom.

"So Penny invited me to her party tonight. She said to bring you guys. What do you think?" I look at each of them, trying to gauge their response. They all glance at each other and it's Rafe who chirps up first.

"A party sounds awesome, I'm in."

"Me too," says JP.

"Sure," says Scott, as he takes my bag off his shoulder and hands it to me.

"Thanks," I say to him.

"Come on, let's get you home. We all know how long it takes you girls to get ready," Rafe laughs, as he playfully taunts me. We all load into the car and JP drops us off one by one and says he will be back to pick us up in a few hours.

When I enter the house, I am in much better spirits than I was earlier.

"Hey Mum," I yell out, trying to find out where she is.

"Hi bub, you sound happy," she says. I'm not sure if she's caught on to my mood or not lately but she hasn't said anything.

"Would it be alright if I went to a party with the guys tonight please?" I beg her. Sometimes she can be a bit hit and miss about parties depending on her own state of mind.

"Are you going with the boys?" she questions.

"Yes, that's what I said."

"Will there be drinking?"

"Ahh yes, probably. But I'll be responsible," I truthfully say, and try to bargain with her.

"Is one of the boys going to be a sober driver? Do I need to ring them to find out?" she says.

"Oh my gosh Mum, please don't ring the guys, that's embarrassing. How about I ring them and ask?" Again with the bargaining.

"Okay, I'll stand right here while you ring," she says, as she crosses her arms over her chest. I guess she's being a responsible parent tonight. I take my phone out of my bag and go to my call log and dial the last one of the guys I'd talked to. He answers after a couple of rings.

"Hey Petal, everything alright?" Rafe asks, worriedly.

"Yeah, I'm okay. I asked Mum about the party and she wanted to know if one of you was going to be a sober driver because I told her we may be drinking," I quickly say. I hear him chuckle through the line.

"Is she standing there with you while you ring?" he asks, and I can hear the amusement in his voice.

"Yes," I say, and he laughs louder.

"Give her the phone, I'll talk to her," he happily says.

"It's for you," I say to my mum, as I hold out my phone for her to take. She grabs it and holds it to her ear. I can't hear what Rafe is saying.

"Oh Rafe, how are you?" Mum says, her cheeks blushing pink and I know Rafe must be putting on the charm. "That's fine, make sure she's not home too late, please." Then she laughs loudly at whatever he says, like a school girl with a crush. "Thank you Rafe," she says, before she hands me the phone with a huge smile on her face.

"All sorted," he says, as I put the phone to my ear. "I'll see you later," he says, and he hangs up. My mum looks at me with a grin across her face. I should think of a name for the spell Rafe has on the opposite sex. The majority of females that come into contact with him go giddy and weak at the knees.

"So can I go?" I ask, because my mum hasn't said anything. She snaps out of her daze to answer me.

"Yes, that's fine bub, as long as you stay with the guys. Rafe said he will be the sober driver for the night and will make sure you get home safely," she says.

"Thanks Mum, you're the best." I lean in and plant a kiss on her cheek.

"Be safe," she says, and I turn around and race up the stairs to find something to wear.

When I enter my room, I take a quick peek at my bedside table drawer, knowing Tate's special notes are in there, hidden from the world. Breathe Tam. I inhale deeply and push the exhale away. While I'm breathing deeply, I push away any thoughts of Tate and the fact it's the third Friday I haven't received a note from him. Fridays are the worst day of the week. I won't admit it out loud but it's the reason I got set off in human bio, knowing another week's gone by without a note from him. I need to accept the fact I won't be getting any more notes. With another deep breath in, I exhale and push away all thoughts of Tate. I need to push him to the side if I'm going to make room to have fun at this party tonight.

After dinner, I have a shower and curl my hair, wanting to put in a bit of effort tonight with my appearance, in the hopes it will lift my spirits. I have music playing in the background to get me in the mood to party. I take my time applying my makeup, thickening my lashes with a couple layers of mascara. I slip on my favourite green dress, hoping the familiarity of it will help boost my confidence for the night. I always had a good time when I've worn this dress in the past. Let's hope the same goes for tonight. I inspect myself in the mirror. The halter dress is a bit loose from the weight I've lost but it still looks quite good on, and it makes me smile at my reflection. I look pretty decent. I finish my look with a nude lippy and some small black heels. Not long after, I hear voices coming from downstairs. I walk and look over the railing and see Rafe in the doorway. I can't hear him with my music playing but he's probably charming my mum if her smile is any giveaway. I grab my bag and walk downstairs.

"Hey Rafe," I say cheerily, hoping my mum doesn't keep us too long. Rafe blatantly looks me up and down, checking me out.

"Looking good Petal. Ready to go?" he says, with a cheeky grin on his face.

"Sure am. I'll see you later Mum," I say, turning towards the door.

"Bye Rafe, and make sure you don't drink. I'm counting on you to keep her safe," she sternly tells Rafe.

"Yes mam," he says, as he salutes her. Yes, he actually salutes her.

"Oh my gosh, you are such a dweeb," I giggle. I tug on his arm and pull him towards JP's car where JP and Scott are waiting for us. Wolf whistling comes from the open windows.

"Wow look at you T, you look amazing," Scott says, beaming at me.

"Thanks," I shyly say, feeling a bit self conscious with all the attention the guys are giving me.

"We will have to fight the guys off with sticks tonight," Scott says, and the others crack up laughing with him.

We fall into easy banter on the way across town to Penny's house. JP twists the cap off a couple of beers and passes them to me and Scott in the back as Rafe is driving. I don't usually like beer but I take it anyway, not caring how I get a buzz going tonight.

"No spewing near the fire pit tonight," JP directs at Scott, laughing.

"Ha ha, very funny," he replies, and the rest of us laugh at his misfortune.

"Now Ice Queen, if any drunk idiots come on to you and we aren't there, do you have any moves you can use?" JP asks me, all amusement gone from his voice.

"You think someone will hit on me?" I ask, feeling a bit nervous now.

"Better to be prepared, just in case," JP says.

"Not really. I've never been in a fight in my life," I tell him.

"You should pick the self-defence class as one of the life skills courses we are starting soon," Rafe says, from the driver's seat.

"If anyone gives you trouble, go straight for the goods and kick them in the nuts," JP says, and I look at the faces of all the guys and see the memory of pain etched on each of them. They all must be remembering a time they've been whacked in the nuts and reliving the pain. It must be as bad as I've heard if it causes the expressions on their faces. I can't help giggling to myself. Hopefully I won't need any nut kicking skills tonight.

As we pull up into Penny's street, Rafe finds an empty spot close to her house. He parks up and kills the engine.

"Skull the rest of your beers and let's go," he tells us. I tip the cool bottle to my lips still having half of it left, while Scott and JP are on their second. I manage to finish it in one go, along with the guys. JP carries the rest of the box, while we get out and walk over to the house. It amazes me how many parties Penny has when her parents are away. It must get pretty lonely, being in this big house by herself all the time.

Scott links his arm with mine, and we follow JP and Rafe to the kitchen where JP places the beer box. He grabs a couple more out and hands one to Scott. I shake my head when he tries to offer me one and grab one of the vodka bottles lying on the table instead. I fill my cup a quarter of the way and top it up with orange juice. Penny's parents know she has parties here and I don't think they care. I've heard rumours they restock their liquor cabinet every time they return from their trips, knowing full well Penny didn't drink all the liquor by herself.

"You made it," I hear from behind me. I take a sip and turn to look at Penny. She's gorgeous in her mid length, sparkling blue dress. Her long, black hair lies straightened down her back.

"Hey Penny," I say, with a genuine smile on my face.

"Cheers," she says, as she presses her plastic cup to mine and we both take a sip giggling.

"Penny, where are all the single girls?" Rafe asks, as he looks around the room trying to find someone to flirt with. Penny has a thoughtful look on her face as she humours Rafe, trying to remember which girls are here she can unleash him on.

"There are a couple outside by the fire pit. I don't think I've heard of you hooking up with them yet," she says, with a cheeky grin directed Rafe's way making me laugh out loud. Rafe looks intrigued and ignores her dig at him.

"Sweet. That is where you guys will find me, if you need me. Petal, will you be okay?" he asks. I look at Penny deciding I will hang out with her and try to make a new girlfriend.

Before I can answer him, Penny jumps in with, "Of course she'll be fine, she's with me," as she links her arm with me, giving Rafe a smile. Satisfied, he leans in giving me a swift kiss to the top of my head then he disappears into the crowd of sweaty people, dancing to the music. I don't know if I'd call it dancing. It's more like animals mating, with the way they are grinding and gyrating their drunk bodies on each other.

Penny sees me watching everyone dancing and asks, "Tamsyn, do you want to dance?"

"I need a few more drinks first," I tell her, laughing.

"Drink up then," she tells me, as she tips her cup up and empties it. JP and Scott are standing to the side talking and laughing with each other and continuing to drink their beers. Penny puts her hands on the kitchen bench behind her and lifts herself up to sit on it. I see her glance at the guys with a curious twinkle in her eye. Interesting. I think she likes the look of one of them.

"So Tamsyn, how come we've never hung out?" she asks.

I drain my cup before I answer, "I was too busy hanging out with bitches, that's why," and we both laugh, knowing exactly who I'm talking about. I push the guys' beer box to the side of the bench and hoist myself up to sit opposite Penny. I grab the vodka and pour a generous amount and then add some orange juice again. Penny holds her cup out for me to fill too, so I do the same with hers.

"Do you usually drink vodka?" I ask her, as I take a sip. She shakes her cup in a small circle to mix it before sipping.

"Yeah, vodka or gin are my go to drink. I drink wine too on occasion," she says.

"Hey T, we might go outside to see what trouble Rafe is getting up to. Do you want to come?" Scott asks.

I look to Penny as I say, "No, I'm going to hang in here with Penny for a bit."

"Cool, if you need us, we will be out the back," Scott says.

"If anyone bothers you, you know what to do," JP tells me, with a serious look on his face and I nod.

They grab a beer and follow each other through the throng of bodies and disappear like Rafe did. As soon as they are out of view, Penny starts laughing in hysterics.

"When did you get three bodyguards and how do I get one?" she asks, which makes me join in her laughter.

"They are a bit protective tonight, I suppose," I say, after the laughter dies down.

"They have every right to be. You look hot, my friend," she says, smiling at me. I hope she is being genuine. I don't want to get sucked into another fake friendship. I don't think I could handle it. I couldn't take another betrayal in my life.

"Thanks," I shyly say to her. "So, where are all your friends?" I ask her, curious as to why she's hanging out with me. Her face drops as she shrugs her shoulders.

"I don't have any close friends. Not any I hang out with constantly. I'm more of a floater," she says quietly. Her remark has me thinking about when I've seen Penny at school. It's true, I always see her with different groups of people. She's one of those people who is friends with everyone but not the same people every day. I see her in a different light now. Is she as lost and alone as I feel most of the time?

"You've got me now," I say to her, hoping I've found a kindred spirit in her. Her wide smile shines at me.

"Okay, drink up so we can go dance." We tip our cups up and finish them off. Refilling our drinks, the vodka gets poured more heavily then topped up with a smidge of orange juice. We link arms and laughing together, we make our way into the pile of sweaty drunk teenagers.

We sway to the music, holding hands with one and grasping our cups in the other. Penny pulls me closer so she can yell in my ear to be heard over the music.

"So is JP single?" she asks, and I can't help but laugh.

"I knew you were checking one of them out. I couldn't tell which one had piqued your interest," I say, laughing as the vodka loosens me up and makes me relax. "I think he's single. I've never seen him with a girl or heard of him having a girlfriend," I tell her, which makes her smile. We get lost in the music and I close my eyes, as I let the euphoria take over.

I don't know how long we are on the dance floor. Every song

glides into the next one, and I can't keep track. Soon Penny is tugging on my hand to get my attention. She holds up her hand with her cup and gestures back towards the kitchen, so keeping a grip on her hand, I follow her lead. I still have a bit of drink in my cup, so I swallow it down and let Penny fill it up for me again. Penny is about to say something, when she looks behind me and her face drops.

"What are you doing here?" she yells over my shoulder, and I turn to see who it's directed at. It's Blake. He's standing right behind me. His eyes are glazed over and he has to lean on the counter to keep his balance. He's wasted. I glance around the room to see if I can locate the guys but they must still be outside. Blake looks me up and down, taking in my appearance.

With a slimy smile he says, "You're looking sexy tonight, Tam," and runs a finger down my arm. Eww, he is gross. How I ever dated him is beyond me.

"What do you want Blake?" I say, letting out a frustrated sigh.

"What? Do you think you're too good for me now or something?" he says, with a menacing voice so far off from the guy I used to date.

"You're the one who cheated on me, remember?" I raise my voice, getting angry with him. I'm angry he has the audacity to come up to me and start something when he was in the wrong. He sneers at me and roughly grabs my arm, dragging me behind him down the hall, off to the side of the house.

"Penny," I call out, panicking as he drags me down the dark deserted hall.

"Tamsyn," I hear Penny yell, before Blake shoves me through an open door into a room. I hear the lock click as he turns and faces me, contempt dripping off his features.

"Blake, you're scaring me," I say, trying to make the guy I dated see sense.

"You should have thought of that before you made me look like an idiot in front of the whole school." He steps closer to me and I back up, hitting the wall.

"Blake, let me out of here," I plead, trying not to let my fear show. He steps right into me, pinning me against the wall with both hands leaning beside my head.

"What happened between us Tam? We were so good together. Let's go back to that," he slurs, as he leans in and sloppily kisses my neck. His split personality is freaking me out. His heavy body presses me into the wall. I try to push him away with my hands but I'm too weak against his drunk strength. I shake, as he roughly grabs my leg and runs his hand up it. For a split second, vivid green eyes cross my vision and I can't control the whimper of his name that leaves me. Wishing he was here to save me. Blake suddenly stops and moves back to look in my eyes.

"Tate?" he roars. "You're calling out for the loser who left you behind? The one who was crying like a baby in the cafeteria?" He lifts his head back and cackles. I don't think I've ever been so disgusted with another person in my life. My brain is foggy from all the vodka but suddenly I remember JP's voice saying, kick him in the nuts.

"He's not coming back for you, Tam. You might as well come back to me. I miss you," he says. He's out of his mind if he believes I would still want to be with him after what he did to me. He leans in again and I use all the strength I can muster, thrusting my knee hard into his balls.

"Aahhh," he screams out in a high pitched voice, dropping to the floor and clutching his private parts. I'm so enraged he thought he could lay his unwanted hands on me. I deliver a swift kick to his ribs too as pounding starts on the door behind me. I turn and stumble to the door, unlocking it. Rafe comes barreling in followed by JP, Scott and Penny. He grabs me by my shoulders, staring into my eyes.

"Did he hurt you Petal?" I shake my head, as he views Blake's body in the foetal position on the bedroom floor.

"Lucky we gave you some tips," JP says, trying to hide his amusement. Rafe doesn't find it funny though and before I can stop him, he has Blake's throat in his hand and he lifts him up one handed. He looked strong but I didn't realise how strong. He throws Blake against the wall, banging his head in the process.

"You disgusting piece of shit. You think you can lay your hands on her and what? She will want you back?" He releases a maniacal laugh. "You touch her, or look in her direction again and I will end you. Understand?"

Blake stares back at him and groans out, "Yep," because Rafe is applying pressure to his throat. He drops Blake and before we register what he's doing, he pulls his fist back and hits Blake right in the nose with a crack. Blood starts streaming down his face and I can't help but feel any sorrow for him. He deserved it. Rafe stands over him so I step forward and place my tiny shaking hand on his arm, gaining his attention.

"Rafe, stop. I'm fine. He didn't hurt me," I say to him, as the anger in his eyes is replaced with worry.

"Are you sure you're okay?" He asks, and I nod.

"Hey, could you guys get everyone out of the house for me please? I don't feel like partying now," Penny says, directing it at JP and Scott. They nod at her and walk out the door.

I hear them both yelling, "Party is over people. Everyone out. Time to go."

Then I hear JP yell to a group who are whining, "If you have a problem with it, take it up with Blake. The slimeball got what was coming to him." His comment shuts them up and I can hear them all shuffling out of the house.

"You okay Tamsyn?" Penny asks, wrapping me in a hug.

"Yeah, I'm fine." Rafe roughly picks the bleeding Blake up by the arm, dragging him out of the room to get him out of the house.

"I'm sorry Tam," Blake murmurs, while holding his bleeding nose in his hands. Rafe stops for a second while I stare at Blake. He betrayed me in the worst possible way and I don't think I can ever forget that. I need to put him behind me if I want to move forward.

"We are done Blake. We were done from the moment you chose to go behind my back with my best friend. So please, if you cared about me at all, you will leave me alone from now on." He doesn't say anything, his glazed eyes boring holes into me so I continue, not sure he got the message. "If you don't leave me alone, I will inform Rafe and next time, I won't stop him," I say, and he visibly shudders as he nods.

"Okay Tam, I hear you loud and clear," he sadly says, as he lets Rafe continue to drag him out of the house.

"You will leave her alone or you'll have a constant broken nose," Rafe threatens him.

Once he's gone Penny turns to me, "I ran to get the guys when I couldn't unlock the door. I was so scared. You should have seen them. As soon as I screamed, 'Tamsyn's in trouble,' they came barging through and pushing people over to get to you. I think I need a bodyguard of my own," she says, as she fans herself and I can't help but laugh. "He didn't do anything to you, did he?" she adds, with worry in her voice.

"No, I kneed him in the nuts before he could. Worst he did was slobber on my neck," I say, shivering.

"Eww, he's disgusting," she says, with a wrinkled nose as she wraps an arm around my shoulder, leading me out of the room. Walking down the now lit up hallway, we enter the kitchen where JP is sitting.

"Everyone is gone. We cleared them all out," JP says.

"Thanks," Penny says, as her cheeks blossom to pink. "Do you guys want a drink?"

"Yeah, me and Scott will take a beer, please Penny," JP says to her, and Penny hands him two beers. He passes one to Scott, who takes a seat after he finishes switching on more of the lights. Penny grabs two untouched plastic cups and fills them with half vodka, half juice and hands one to me.

Rafe walks in the front door wiping his hands against each other and says, "The trash has been taken out," and pulls out the seat next to me to sit down. "He won't bother you again Tamsyn. If he looks or breathes in your direction, let me know and I'll sort him out," he kindly says, hitting my shoulder gently with his own.

"Thanks so much Rafe," I say, extremely grateful I have the guys as friends. I don't know what I'd do without them. Penny stands up and starts hunting around in her freezer. Pulling out a bag of frozen peas, she wraps it in a tea towel and passes it to Rafe.

"Here, for your hand," she tells him, with a small smile. Rafe inspects his hand, flexing it and wincing. His knuckles are red too. He places the homemade ice pack against his hand, holding it in place with the other one.

"You did a lot of damage with one punch," I say to Rafe, inspecting his hand.

He scratches his head and says, "Umm, I may have taken a few extra shots to his body as I threw him out of the house. Just making sure my message got across." I shake my head at him, smiling. We all sip our drinks silently, lost in our own thoughts.

"I think I shouldn't host any parties for a while," Penny says, as she looks into her half finished cup.

"Don't let Blake put you off Pen. If you want to have parties here, keep it discrete. Or don't let in idiots like Blake," JP says to her, and her cheeks turn from a slight pink to a dark red. I look down at my own cup, hiding my smile at the use of the name Pen. I've never heard anyone call her anything other than Penny. I glance her way and she's looking at me, her smile widening. She's thinking the exact same thing. She must like the nickname.

"Since the party turned into a bust and it's still early, do you guys want to watch a movie?" Penny asks us, looking around at the group. The guys stare at me, letting me know it's my call, as their parents don't give them curfews or anything. They pretty much come and go as they please. The joys of being a teenage boy, I guess. I glance at the clock behind me on the kitchen wall, and see it's not quite eleven o'clock yet.

"Yeah, let's watch a movie. One won't hurt," I say, hopping up from my seat. The guys follow as I stumble over to the couches in the lounge. I get sandwiched between Rafe and Scott. JP sits on the other couch, while Penny follows, after grabbing the vodka from the bench.

"Hold up," JP says, and jumps up, walks into the kitchen and comes back with the remaining box of beers. We all look at him with raised brows. "If the girls are going to keep drinking, then so am I," he states, and we all chuckle. Penny grabs the remote and sets up Netflix.

"Any requests?" she asks, as she scans through the selection of movies.

"Anything with hot babes is fine by me," Rafe chimes in.

She stops on a choice and Rafe says, "Yeah, that's good with me. I should get the final say as I'm the sober driver." We all laugh and settle in to watch Charlie's Angels. Penny takes a seat by JP and I peek at her out of the corner of my eye. She's sitting on the edge of the seat, stiff as can be. JP notices her awkwardness too.

"Pen, move back next to me, you're blocking the T.V," JP says, as he slides his arm along the back of their couch.

"Sorry," she softly says, as she wriggles back against the couch leaving space between them.

"Penny, can you top up my drink please?" I say, handing my drink to Scott, who passes it to JP to hold out for Penny. She fills it up along with her own and then they pass the cup back down the line to me. We all relax and get comfortable as Penny gets up and switches off the lounge light. I slowly sip my drink while getting engrossed in the movie. The last thing I remember is Cameron Diaz holding a bad guy's throat with her foot and wishing I was a badass like her. If I was, Blake wouldn't have been able to do anything to me tonight. Those self-defence lessons are sounding like a great idea now.

"Sweet dreams," I hear, softly whispered in my ear.

"Tate?" I ask, through the hazy fog of sleep and vodka.

I hear a soft sigh and then, "No Petal, it's Rafe. You're in your bed now. Safe and sound. Get some sleep."

"Rafe?" I ask, sighing.

"Yeah Petal?" he replies.

"Why wasn't I enough?" And as the floodgates open, the tears unleash freely down my face.

"Aww Petal, come here," Rafe softly says into the dark, pulling me out from under the blankets and wrapping me into his warm arms.

In between sobs I ask, "Why wasn't I enough for Blake when he had me? He had to cheat on me behind my back for months. And Tate. Why wasn't I enough to make him come back?" Rafe squeezes me tightly and holds me together while I fall apart.

"You know what I think? Blake is a total moron and you deserve so much better than him. Don't give him a second thought, he's not worth it. Okay?" he asks into the dark. I nod against his chest and he knows I've heard him. "I know Tate cares about you. He can't see it right now because he's blinded by his grief. I don't want you to ever think you are not good enough. You are amazing and any guy would be lucky to call you his. So don't you forget it." His words slow my tears, and I manage to calm myself down. Rafe lays me back down in my bed and tucks the covers up to my chin, pressing the blanket in at the sides. He says quietly, "Snug as a bug in a rug," before his weight leaves the bed.

"Night Rafe. Thank you for rescuing me," I say, before he walks out my bedroom door.

"Any time. Sweet dreams, Tamsyn," he whispers back, as he leaves the room. I fold my arms around my waist, hoping to hold myself together the way Rafe did moments ago. Luckily the vodka is still swimming in my system so it isn't long before I drift back to sleep.

-- Tate --

I don't know what day it is and I don't care. I leave my room only to go to the toilet and to eat. I spend the majority of my time in my bed, listening to music and sleeping. My world has been a blur since the funeral. Mum and Dad have tried and failed to get me to leave the house. I don't have the energy. I'm exhausted all the time. JP and his dad left a few days after the funeral. I won't admit it out loud but I miss JP. I've been a terrible friend and cousin to him. I didn't say goodbye to him. It's easier this way. I had to push him and Tamsyn away. They don't deserve this and they shouldn't have to deal with my issues. Especially Tamsyn. I ache for her but as soon as it arises, I have to push it down. I can't feel that way about her now. I'm no good for her. She deserves better than me. I was stupid to think I could help her. I didn't fix her, I made her hurt worse. As I'm lying on my bed, staring up at the ceiling, a text comes through. I grab my phone and open it up.

Rafe: Hey dude. Call Tamsyn. She needs you.

My heart thunders in my chest. I hate hearing her name because it makes me feel. I don't have the energy to deal with it, but I need to know if she's alright.

Tate: Is everything ok?

I tap my index finger on the side of my phone, waiting anxiously for his reply.

Rafe: Blake locked her in a room with him at a party.

Before I finish reading the text, I'm ringing Rafe while my heart drums a hole into me.

"What happened?" I yell into the phone, as soon as he answers.

"Hey man, Blake dragged her into a room at Penny's and locked the door. I don't know exactly what happened. She wouldn't say. She did say he didn't hurt her. She looked shaken up though," he explains. I can hear my laboured breathing when he stops talking.

"Is she alright? When was this?" I ask. My heart aches because I wasn't there to protect her from him.

"It was last night. By the time we got in the room, she had kicked him in the nuts and he was on the ground. I broke his nose again so I'm hoping he doesn't have the nerve to try anything else." I can hear the anger in his voice coming through the receiver. My blood boils and my misplaced emotions come out as anger at Rafe.

"Where were you guys? Why weren't you with her?" I yell at him, which I know he doesn't deserve but I can't control myself.

"Dude, you're the one who left her behind. Don't get mad at me when we are still here, trying to pick up the pieces," Rafe yells back, and it makes me feel worse because he's right. I did choose to walk away from her. I have no right to be angry right now.

"I'm sorry. I didn't mean that. I'm just worried," I tell him.

"She's drinking more now. And the times when I've been with her, she gets so smashed she falls asleep. I've got to sneak her back into her house without her mum noticing and get her into bed." I can't handle his words, they're piercing my soul. I'm supposed to be numb but any mention of her and she cracks me in half, making me bleed. This is why I can't be with her. She makes me feel too much. "And do you want to know the sad part?" No I don't but my curious mind asks, before my heart can stop it.

"What's the sad part?" I ask, knowing I won't be able to handle the answer.

"She whispers your name when I tuck her in, thinking it's you instead of me," he sadly says, and my heart shatters into a thousand pieces. Hurting from leaving the only girl I want, but hurting more, knowing I can't go back to her. I'm not good for her and I don't want to feel this pain she brings out of me. I need to contain it.

"I can't Rafe," I plead with him, hoping he will understand what I'm trying to say.

He lets out a sad sigh before he says, "I didn't take you for a coward, Tate. I hope you wake up one day soon and realise what a huge mistake you are making before it's too late. She's a great girl and she deserves happiness. I know you are grieving for your sister but Tamsyn needs you." And with that, the line goes dead.

"No, she doesn't deserve this. She deserves better," I say into the dead line, and set my phone back beside my bed. Both JP and Rafe have said Tamsyn needs me now but I can't. I lie back and stare at the ceiling. I wipe the wetness from my cheeks not realising I was crying. Don't think Tate. Don't think. I focus on my breathing, bringing it back to a normal level before a panic attack occurs. I turn my numb switch up and push away the girl who I convince myself I don't need at all. I wish I was smart enough to tell myself how wrong I am.

The next day rolls around and the knocking on my bedroom door pulls me away from my ceiling. Mum and Dad's heads pop around it, asking if they can come in. I stare at them blankly.

"Tate, me and your mother have been talking. We think it's time you went back to school," Dad says.

"I told you, I don't want to go back and live with JP," I tell them, frustrated they aren't listening to me and I'm having to tell them again.

"No honey, you misunderstand. We think you should go back to school here. Your old school," Mum says.

"I can't," I say, looking at Mum, knowing she is the easier one to plead with. Dad moves into the room and sits at the end of the bed.

"Son, you can't keep going on like this. Quinn wouldn't want this." Hearing her name irks me and I explode.

"You don't know what she'd want and she isn't here to tell us, so I don't think she should come into this conversation," I yell. I'm sick of people telling me what Quinn would want. They have no idea what she'd want or how she'd feel. If they did then maybe she would still be with us and I wouldn't have to feel like this.

"Fine. Me and your mother can't handle this," he yells back, waving his hand around my room. "We can't have you going down the same path as Quinn." His last words have me stopping my retaliation and looking at them properly for the first time in a while. Mum stands there, wringing her hands with unshed tears behind her eyes while Dad looks exhausted. I don't want to cause them more pain.

"Whatever. I'll go back to school then," I tell them, accepting defeat. They don't need to be worrying about me at the moment.

Mum smiles sadly towards me and softly says, "I'll get your old uniform together honey and you can go tomorrow. No point in putting it off. There's not much left of the term so it'll be a good start."

She looks afflicted so I smile back at her and reply, "Sure Mum, that would be great. Thanks." She leaves the room in search of my uniform and Dad stands up to leave.

He turns to me as he grips the door and says, "It will be better once you get back into the swing of things." Then he walks away, closing the door behind him. I don't know who he's trying to convince. Me or him. I lie back down and wonder how I'm going to face the school that holds so many memories of Quinn.

Sleep doesn't come. Images of scared, blue eyes keep sleep from taking hold. I spend most of the night staring into the darkness. My eyes finally close in the early hours of the morning and before I know it, Mum is knocking on my door waking me up for school. I drag myself from my bed and go to the bathroom to relieve myself. Afterwards I stagger into the kitchen to make up a supersized, strong cup of coffee. I'm going to need a lot of caffeine to get through the day. I make black coffee with no sugar. I don't find enjoyment in what was once my favourite drink. There's no point in sprucing it up with milk or sugar either. I only need it for the caffeine hit now, so black will do. I add some cold water so I can gulp it down without having to wait, needing the energy to get ready for school.

I declined my dad's offer to drive me to school. He probably doesn't think I will go to school but I'm dressed and walking there, if only to prove him wrong. It's not like I have anything better to do. The closer I get to school, the more kids I notice walking too. A few I recognise and I instantly see the pity on their faces, they don't try to hide it. This is exactly what I don't need right now. I take a deep breath and prepare myself for all the sad looks I will have directed my way today. If I fake being happy, hopefully they will keep their pitying looks to themselves.

I have to go to the school office to sort out my classes as I didn't start the school year here. I don't care what classes they put me in. As I enter the gate, I feel the familiar increase of my heart rate and breathe in and out slowly. Being back here without Quinn is making my flight response awaken. I will not let it take hold this time. I need to push through this or I will always be running away. It takes me a few minutes, standing frozen while I get myself under control, before I can continue on. With a slow exhale, I walk to the office, avoiding the stares I knew I'd receive. The school principal Mr. Sinclair greets me as I walk in.

"Hi Tate," he says, extending his hand for me to shake. "Your mother gave me a call this morning and said you would be back. I told her I'd personally help you sort out your classes. So why don't you come into my office and we can get started?" I don't say anything as I walk into the room behind him. I take the seat opposite his immaculately clean desk as he sits behind it. He swings around in his chair and shuffles through a pile of papers situated behind him. He grabs what he needs and swings back towards me. "So Tate, it's late into the school year but we will try to get you into the classes you want, where we can. Now are there any particular classes you want to be in?" he asks, as he raises his eyes to look at me.

I could care less which classes I get put in but before I can answer, an image of blue eyes cross my vision and I find myself saying, "Human biology. I'd like to be in that class if I could please." I plaster a fake smile on my face, to cover the sadness momentarily trying to infiltrate me.

"Human bio, okay let me have a look," Mr. Sinclair says, as he scans over the papers in his hands. After a moment he leans forward to show me the timetable and the subjects he's highlighted, to indicate where he could fit me in. "Okay Tate. I can get you into human bio, as long as you don't mind taking either geography or classical studies," he says.

"Classics will do," I say, as I don't mind English and it's closer to English than geography would be.

"And can you pick between P.E and art?" he asks, highlighting the classics periods on the timetable.

"P.E," I tell him, not having an artistic bone in my body. At least if I'm doing P.E, it might help to exhaust me so I can sleep at night.

"Great," he says, smiling at me as he continues with his

highlighting. "There we go. All done. That worked out well," he says, and I nod as the classes aren't too bad. He passes me the timetable then leans back in his chair. "Now Tate, if you are having trouble with anything or if you need someone to talk to, please come and see me. My door is always open. I know you've had a hard time of late and I'm here to help you with anything you need," he rambles on.

Taking a leaf out of Tamsyn's book, I turn the fake smile right up and say, "Thanks Mr. Sinclair, I'll remember that." Then I stand to leave, with my schedule in hand.

"I won't keep you any longer. I don't want you to be late on your first day back."

"Thanks again, Sir," I say, as I hurry out of there. Glancing at my schedule, I check to see what my first lesson of the day will be and what do you know, it's human bio.

I know this school like the back of my hand so I make it to class in record time. It's twice the size of JP's school so you would think I could walk around unnoticed but that doesn't happen. I avoid eye contact with everyone I pass, not wanting to hear their condolences or heartfelt sympathies. I haven't crossed paths with Xander or Pierce yet. I didn't text them to let them know I'd be at school so they are in for a surprise. I'm sure I will run into them eventually. I open the door to the class and I'm greeted by Mrs. Browne, my old science teacher.

"Aww Tate, it's lovely to see you back at school. I was devastated to hear about Quinn. How are you holding up?" she asks, as she leans forward and grasps both my hands in hers.

"I'm fine," I tell her, wanting this conversation to end as soon as possible. Her eyes bore into me and for a minute, I think she might say something else but she lets it go. When people ask how I am, I don't believe they want an honest answer. Would they look at me weird if I said I'm drowning, and the waves keep dragging me out to sea to continue their torture. My only true friend is the darkness I use to keep me numb so I don't feel, because if I feel then I will completely crumble and I don't think I will survive. I fear my heart will stop working. It can't possibly handle this amount of pain. It physically hurts at times, so I have to keep it contained or I wouldn't make it through each day. What would she say if that was my answer?

"There's a spare seat down the back, if you'd like to take that. If you are having trouble with anything, please come and see me so we can catch you up," she kindly says. I direct a small smile her way and then hurry to my seat. I packed all the books that I'd already been using this year. Mum wanted to buy me all new things yesterday but I said there was no point. I could make do with what I had already. I search my bag for my human bio book and pull it out. I flip through the pages to find a new blank one to start on.

As I'm flipping, I'm interrupted by Mrs. Browne instructing the class, "Welcome class to a new week. This week we are going to be focussing on the structure of the eyeball." My careless flipping stops, as a memory of Tamsyn dissecting the eye flicks through my vision. She looked ridiculously cute, grossed out by the fluid leaking out of the eye. I shake my head, ridding myself of thoughts of her. That's not what I need right now. I glance down at my book in my hands and see I'm at the page that she wrote her number on. I can't get away from her. I run my thumb across her writing, the same way I would rub my thumb across her hand to comfort her. Maybe it wasn't only her I was comforting but myself too. I lay my head on my arms and continue to run my thumb back and forth across the page, needing a link to her to keep me from falling apart. Don't think Tate. Don't think. Don't think. Don't think.

It isn't until lunch that Xander sees me on my way to the cafeteria. He comes up and puts out his hand for a fist bump so I return it.

"Hey man, why didn't you tell us you were coming back to school? I could have picked you up this morning," he says, happy to see me.

"Sorry Xan, it was a last minute decision to come today. I wanted to psyche myself up to get back into school mode, that's why I walked.

Feel free to pick me up from now on though," I tell him, with fake enthusiasm.

"Sweet, I'll pick you up tomorrow," he says. "Let's find Pierce. I'm starving," he adds, as he exaggerates, rubbing his belly. He opens the door to the cafeteria, holding it for me to walk through first. As soon as I enter, it's like the whole school zones in on me and silence ensues. You could hear a fricken pin drop. I grind my teeth, keeping myself under control and turn my back on the crowd and face Xander.

"So anything new with you?" I ask him, hoping if I divert my attention to him, everyone else will forget I'm here.

"Not really. I was seeing this girl from out of town for a bit but it was too much work with her living so far away. Unfortunately, it fizzled out. On the bright side, at least I found out long distance relationships are not for me," he tells me, laughing. My mind flickers to the girl who is so far away but has ownership of my heart, and a pang goes through me. I rub my chest to rid myself of the feeling quickly, before he notices his words affect me. He spots Pierce as he walks into the cafeteria behind a few other people.

"Pierce, look who I found," he calls out to him, gaining a few looks from the crowded room. Pierce's face lights up when he sees me.

"Tate!" he yells, as he jogs the couple of steps it takes to get to me. He wraps me up in a big one armed hug, not caring if people are staring. I've been a lousy friend of late. These guys have been my best friends since I was little, and I ignored them when I moved to stay with JP. I forgot about my life here. I pushed my old life out of my head so I wouldn't have to think. Especially about Quinn. I found it easier to cope that way.

"Hey," I say back to him, returning his hug.

"You good?" he asks, with worry behind his eyes.

I shrug as I say laughing, "It's school. It's not like I'm going to be singing from the chandeliers, now am I?" Both of them join in my laughter but I catch a glimpse of concern crossing Pierce's face before it's gone. I was always closer with Pierce, so I know it will probably be harder for me to fool him into thinking everything is fine. As we line up to fill our trays with food, Pierce taps me on the shoulder.

"So have you seen Avery yet?" Pierce whispers. I take a deep inhale calming myself before I answer.

"No I haven't. How has she been?" I don't want to know the answer. I want to change the subject quickly but I don't know how.

"She's been crying around school every day. I'm not sure she's handling it. I thought I'd give you a heads up, before you run into her," he says.

"Thanks man," I say, not entirely thankful. I've mindlessly loaded my tray with food while I was talking with him, not taking notice of what I was grabbing. Luckily I'm not fussy and I don't have any food allergies to worry about. The news that my sister's best friend is a mess, made me go into autopilot. The fact I was hooking up with her, behind my sister's back, for a few weeks before her suicide attempt makes me sick. I'm hoping I can delay seeing her for a while. That's one can of worms I don't want to open.

For once, luck is on my side and I don't see any sign of Avery for the whole day. Guess that's the good thing about going to such a big school. I'm sure I won't be able to avoid her forever. One of her friends, no doubt, has probably already filled her in on my return. Hooking up with Avery is one of my biggest regrets. She and Quinn had been best friends for the last few years. They'd always hung out in the same group but only in the last few years did they get a bit closer. Avery was always around at our house and it was clear to everyone, she had a crush on me. She didn't try to hide it. I didn't take much notice of her because I didn't want to go out with my sister's best friend and have something happen, potentially wrecking their friendship. It wasn't until I got drunk at a party about six months ago, she hit on me and something happened. I was too out of it to fend her off like I usually did. For a second I was weak and gave in. I was lonely and I didn't want to push her away. She is gorgeous but she knows it and flaunts it. She has long light brown hair with blonde highlights through it. She could be a model with her height and figure. Her dark brown, almond eyes are always framed with perfect makeup. I can't remember what she looks like without her face done up.

For a few weeks after the party, we were sneaking around behind Quinn's back. Pierce only knew what was going on as he'd seen us hooking up at the party. She got a bit too intense, too quickly and more demanding, the more we hooked up so I decided to cool things. It is exactly what I didn't want happening. She wanted to have sex but I was not going to let my first time be with my sister's best friend. I'd told her one day at school that we couldn't see each other any more. I thought she was fine with it but she kept flirting with me and being a bit too handsy. She kept texting me so I had to set her straight. I don't know why she couldn't get it through her head. It was like she kept hoping I would change my mind. That was a few days before Quinn took all the pills. I saw her at the funeral but I kept my distance. Pretty sure I won't be able to keep her away from me forever.

Xander gives me a ride home from school and reminds me he will be there in the morning to pick me up. Pierce plays in a few different school sports teams so usually has some training after school, so he very rarely rides home with us. I enter the house and my mum is there, like I suspected she would be.

"How was school? Did you get into the classes you wanted?" she asks.

"Yeah, it was fine, Mum. Classes are fine," I say with a flat tone, my only thought is getting to my room as fast as possible to avoid the third degree.

"That's great, Tate. I knew it would be good for you to get back to school," she says, relief flooding her voice. I scurry to my room and close the door. I flop on my bed and let the exhaustion of the day take over.

It's tiring pretending everything is fine and I'm happy. Life in general is tiring. I don't know how Tamsyn did it for so long.

A vibration in my pocket grabs my attention. It's a text but I see the name on the screen and choose to put my phone down, not opening it. The can of worms can stay firmly shut for another day.

Chapter 6

-- Tate --

I manage to avoid Avery all of Tuesday morning, but my luck runs out and she catches up with me at lunch time.

"Tate," I hear her squeal, as she sees me in the cafeteria, drawing attention to herself. She runs up to me, flinging herself into my stiff arms and before I can peel her off of me, I hear her whimpering into my shoulder. People are staring at us so I wrap my arms around her, not wanting to appear callous. I feel a grip on my shoulder and angle my head to see who it is, and I lock eyes with a sympathetic Pierce. He is the only person who knows how hard it was to let Avery down the first time so he feels my pain.

"It's okay Avery," I tell her, as I lead her over to a table and find a seat so I can disengage from her. I sit her down and take the seat opposite her. Funny, for someone who was supposed to be crying, her makeup is still flawless. No hint of redness in her eyes either, they're still as white as ever. My guard goes up and I suspect someone is using my sister's death to get sympathy from me, something I can't stand.

"You're fine now Avery," I say, clenching my jaw and tearing myself out of her clutches.

"It's been so horrible, Tate. I've been a mess," she says, wiping away a non-existent tear from her eye. "Did you get my text? I heard from Monique you were back at school," she says, trying to change the subject. I still haven't opened her text. To be honest, I had completely forgotten about it.

"No, I didn't," I lie. Her face drops but she quickly regathers herself. She leans forward, sticking her tits out, and runs a sharp fingernail over my hand.

"When I heard you were back, I thought we could pick up where we left off," she says, in what I assume is supposed to be a seductive voice. My eyes roam over this gorgeous girl and I feel nothing. She's beautiful on the outside but that's it. I have no feelings towards her. My heart is too broken to feel anything right now. Yeah right, more like I left my heart behind with the blue eyed fairy in the green dress, and I don't know how to function without her. I'll keep telling myself it's because I'm broken. The lie is much easier to swallow than the truth.

"Avery, I already told you I couldn't be with you," I tell her, not caring if I hurt her feelings at this point. I only want to get away from her.

"We can help each other through our grief Tate. We're both hurting," she says, trying a different angle but I'm not buying it.

"No Avery. I'm not the same person I was," I say standing, because if I don't get away soon, I will snap at her and it's not something I want to do in front of a crowd.

She must see it's a losing battle so she says, "Fine Tate, I just thought we could be there for each other. If you ever need me, you know where to find me." She hastily pulls out her chair and leaves the cafeteria.

I join the end of the line, grab a tray of food and locate Pierce and Xander seated at a table by the window. I weave my way through the scattered tables to join them.

"Did you manage to dodge the bullet?" Pierce asks, holding in his laughter and I roll my eyes. Xander glances between us. His eyes light up when it clicks into place.

"You and Avery?" he quietly shrieks my way.

"Keep it down, would you?" I tell him, as I take a bite from my apple. While I chew the piece in my mouth I say, "There's no me and Avery. It was over before it began."

"You didn't sleep with her, did you?" Xander asks, as his nose wrinkles in disgust.

"No I didn't. Still got my V plates," I say emotionless, and they both laugh at me.

"I can't believe you are still hanging onto It man. You're seventeen. Don't you think it's about time you gave it up already? Not to Avery but someone?" Xander questions.

"Leave him alone Xan. You know he wants it to be special with the magical princess he keeps wishing for," Pierce says, and they both crack up with laughter.

"Green fairy," I mutter before I can stop myself, and they laugh louder.

"Sorry, my mistake. It's a magical green fairy from a fairy tale land he's waiting for," Pierce says, as they cackle with laughter. They know I've been waiting for someone special for years now. What they don't know is I have already found her, and I left her behind.

-- Tamsyn --

The guys have increased their protective factor by a thousand percent. Someone is always walking with me to my classes. I am sure they have enlisted the help of Penny too because she walks with me when I know the boys' classes are on the other side of the school. They would be late if they had to take me to my class and then race back to theirs. I understand them not wanting me to be on my own, in case Blake tries something but I highly doubt he will. I'm pretty sure he got the message, loud and clear. His nose is all bruised and it runs under his eyes. Thick strips of white bandage cover his nose, making him look like he had a nose job. Every time he sees me, he whips around and high tails it in the other direction. I notice Parker, Chloe and Leyla all still sit with him at lunch. It doesn't look like him and Leyla are a couple though. I have a feeling he dumped her as soon as the excitement and novelty wore off. I've heard whispers from people saying he got his nose broken because he was forcing himself on a girl at Penny's party. No one saw it was Rafe who punched him thankfully. If they had, I'm sure they would come to the conclusion I was the girl and no one has said anything to me about it yet. I hope it stays this way. I've had enough drama this year at school already, I don't need any more.

The past few days I've been going through the motions and not engaging in class. I'm still feeling lost without Tate. I want to text him but I stop myself before I do. I don't think my heart can handle any more rejection from him. I'm not sure if the guys have heard from him either. They don't mention him so neither do I. It's like an unspoken rule with our friendship now. Nobody mention Tate or you will face the firing squad.

Since the party on Friday, Penny has moved seats and taken up the seat next to me in English. The seat Tate once occupied. She's fast becoming a good friend of mine. It's nice to have a girl around, instead of only the guys to talk to. Sometimes a girl needs some good girl talk.

So this is where I find myself on Wednesday in English, sitting between Scott and Penny.

"Hey, would you want to come over to my house after school?" Penny whispers to me, while Mr. Barnes blabbers on about something I am not paying attention to.

"Sure, what did you want to do?" I whisper back.

"Could watch some Netflix and binge on junk?" she asks.

"Sounds perfect," I say, smiling at her. "Can I catch a ride home with you and you drop me off later?" I ask, because I can't drive and I don't have a car.

"Yeah sure, that's fine" she says, smiling.

Scott overhears our conversation and whispers, "Can I come?" pleading at us with his best puppy dog eyes.

"No. I need some girl time," I tell him, holding in my laughter at his sad face so Mr. Barnes doesn't catch us talking.

"I could be an honorary girl," he beseeches, and I have to cover my mouth to stop the giggles from spilling over.

"Next time," I say, once I've calmed myself enough to speak.

"Fine," he says, pouting.

After school, I walk with Penny over to JP's car to fill the guys in on my plan. None of them look happy to be excluded from my plans. It's not like I hang out with them out of school all the time.

"How about I make it up to you guys by having a sleepover on Friday?" I tell them, trying to cheer them up, and it works.

"Cool with me," Rafe says.

"Sounds good," Scott says.

JP chimes in with, "Sweet." I say my goodbyes and walk away with Penny.

When we are out of ear shot she says, "Did I hear that right? You have sleepovers together?" She looks at me, with a questioning stare.

"Yeah, it's a long story," I say, not used to having to explain me and the guys' situation before.

She links her arm with me and says, "Lucky we have all afternoon then." I quickly flick a text to my mum before I hop in Penny's car. I let her know I've gone to a friend's house and I'll be home later. I don't want her worrying.

As we sit on her couch, taking turns painting each others' toenails, I fill her in on how me and the guys became friends. I also spill my guts and tell her all about Tate.

"Aww Tamsyn, you know what I think?" she says, after she's listened to everything I told her.

"What?" I am desperate to hear another girl's opinion on the situation.

"I think he's hurting from losing his sister and didn't know what he was doing. You know what it's like to lose someone close to you. You can't think clearly, let alone make rational decisions when it's all so raw. Give him time. I'm sure he will come around," she says. Hearing it from another girl makes my heart lighter.

"You think so?" I ask, hopeful.

"I know so. Plus who could resist you? You're hot, girlfriend," she says, and we both crack up laughing.

"And if he doesn't come back, I will help you find another hunk to sink your teeth into," she says, winking at me. My heart throbs at the thought of not being with Tate, but I quickly push the thought aside and choose to laugh with Penny instead.

"Now, fill me in on everything about JP," she says, with a twinkle in her eye. This girl has it bad.

We spend the rest of the afternoon gossiping about people at school and I tell her everything of importance I can think of, when it comes to JP. Which I must say isn't much. I will have to put my sleuthing skills to work and get some juicy information out of him, without him suspecting. Most of my time with the guys had been so focussed on Tate I hadn't gotten to know the guys on a deeper level. This needs to change.

She puts on Ten Things I Hate About You and we binge on popcorn and chocolate before she drops me home. I fall asleep in bed, thinking it was the best day I've had in a long time. I wish they could all be this good.

Don't Panic. Keep Breathing.

Chapter 7

-- Tamsyn --

It's Friday night and as promised, I have organised for the guys to come around for a sleepover. So here they are, setting up the mattresses on my floor in their usual spots. I don't know when to drop my bombshell. I guess now is as good a time as any.

"Sooo I… ummm… invited Penny to our sleepover," I say quietly, while biting my lip. They turn my way and then glance at each other.

Scott shrugs and Rafe says, "That's fine with us. We like Penny." Their response has my mouth popping open. "You might want to close your mouth Petal before a bug flies in," Rafe adds, and they all laugh as one. "Are you shocked we don't mind?" he asks after he calms down.

"To be honest, yes. We haven't had any new people in our group for a while and I wasn't sure if you guys would mind her crashing the sleepover. I asked her before I thought about what you guys might think," I say in a rush, taking a big breath once I'm finished.

Rafe comes over, stands in front of me and grabs both my

shoulders saying, "We like that you've made a new friend and Penny is cool. Any time you want to include her, feel free to." I can't help but smile in response. I'm lucky these guys have stuck by me through everything.

"Tamsyn, someone is at the door for you," my mum calls from downstairs, so I leave the guys to finish off and skip down the stairs to greet Penny. She's standing there in a black tank top and matching sleep shorts with skull bones on them. She has black fluffy slippers on her feet, her hair in pigtail plaits and is hugging a pillow to her chest with a bag slung over her shoulder. Man, she looks good even in pajamas. She makes me feel so skinny next to her perfect hourglass figure.

"Oh my gosh, aren't you the cutest sleepover buddy," I say, and it earns a smile from her.

"I haven't been to a sleepover in forever," she says, biting her fingernails.

"I'm glad you came," I say, smiling at her. "Mum, this is my friend Penny. Penny, this is my mum," I say, gesturing between them.

"Hi Penny, it's nice to meet you."

"Hi Mrs. Winter, thanks for having me," Penny says, swaying side to side.

"You can call me Tanya. Honestly, it's no trouble at all. Especially with the boys here. You would think they would be rowdy but they are surprisingly quite tame," Mum says.

"Come Penny, let's go up to my room," I say, as I take the bag off her shoulder and carry it for her. We start the trek up the stairs and I notice Penny glancing around, admiring my house.

"Thanks for inviting me Tamsyn," she says quietly, before we hit the top of the stairs. I can tell it means a lot to her. I still don't understand how this lovely girl doesn't have any close friends. It's a good thing we found each other.

"It's no problem at all," I say, and I lead her to my room where I can hear the guys already debating about which movie to start with. When we enter, I fake a cough to get their attention. As soon as they lay eyes on Penny, it's dead quiet as they all ogle her with their eyes. She squirms under their blatant perusal of her and I can't blame her. I'm starting to feel a bit uncomfortable too.

"Umm guys, eyes up here," I say, as I point my fingers at my eyes, hoping they understand. Rafe drops his head and rubs his forehead, Scott turns a bright pink which stretches all the way down his neck and JP smirks, not caring he got caught checking Penny out.

"Sorry," Rafe and Scott say together, but again JP stands there not saying a word. He doesn't look sorry at all. I should play matchmaker with Penny and JP. They both seem to like each other. I thought it was Rafe I would have to worry about but because she's my friend, he sees her as a no go zone. The guys have never looked at me like that but then my mind flickers to Tate. He's probably the reason they don't look at me other than a friend. It wouldn't feel right anyway, I think of them like brothers.

"We were just trying to decide on a movie," Scott pipes in, trying to change the subject and rid the room of the awkwardness.

"What's it between?" I ask.

"John Wick or The Notebook," Rafe says, and then he cheekily smiles at Penny and says, "Penny, if you can guess which one was my pick then you can choose the movie."

She glances at the rest of us like it's a trap, and then hesitantly says, "John Wick?"

"Err wrong. One thing you need to know about me Penny. I'm a lover not a fighter, unless I'm dealing with trash. I love me some romance movies. And hot babes. Always hot babes," he says, and we all bend over laughing. Rafe always knows how to break the ice. "So The Notebook it is. We can watch John Wick afterwards," he says happily, as he gets his way.

"Penny, you can sleep in the bed with me," I tell her. "Oh, come with me and I'll show you where the bathroom is." She follows me out of the room and down the hall as the guys finish sorting the movie. Scott runs downstairs to hunt for snacks. "Here's the bathroom," I say, gesturing towards it. "Are you okay?" I whisper to her, in case the guys can overhear us.

"Am I dressed okay?" she says, pulling on her sleep shorts, trying to magically make them longer.

"You look fine, Penny. It's not your fault you look hot when you go to sleepovers," I say, covering my giggles with my hand.

"Oh my gosh Tamsyn, I nearly died when they were all staring at me. When I dress up for my parties, I don't get looks like that," she says, and we bend over giggling some more.

"You should start wearing your pajamas to parties instead," I say between our laughs, and we turn to walk back to the room.

Before we enter the room, I lean close into Penny and cover my mouth so the guys can't see and whisper in her ear, "Now don't gawk at the guys when they take off their shirts to sleep." With a wide smile on my face, I skip into the room and jump into bed, looking over at a frozen Penny in the doorway. I can't help but laugh at the wide eyes on her face. "Come on Penny, into bed," I say, patting the space next to me where I put her pillow. She shakes her head, hurries over and pulls the cover over her lap. I feel her fingers give my thigh a pinch. I let out a squeal and it has her laughing.

"Hey, keep it down you two," Rafe says, smiling from where he's standing in front of the T.V, trying to find The Notebook.

Scott comes in with his arms piled full of snacks and drops them on the bed in front of me and Penny. I snatch the gummy aeroplanes before the guys can steal them. Penny holds back, watching the guys as they take their favoured snacks, leaving the rest in front of me and her. JP flicks off the light and pushes the door so it's wide open, how my mum likes it. Rafe is the first to take off his shirt and his pants follow, leaving his boxers on. JP takes his shirt off but chooses to sleep in his basketball shorts. Scott leaves both his t-shirt and shorts on, hopping into his makeshift bed as he is.

I nudge Penny with my arm and whisper, "You've got some drool here." I touch the side of my mouth, trying to keep my laughter from escaping. She nudges me back and we fall back onto our pillows in a fit of giggles.

"You two better not be giggling the whole movie," I hear Rafe say from his mattress, but I hear the smile in his voice and know he's happy I've made a new friend. So we snuggle down into the bed, devouring our treats and for once, I manage to stay up and watch two movies, enjoying every minute of it.

-- Tate --

I can't sleep. I never can these days. My mind runs in circles, wired and tired at the same time but it won't let me sleep. It doesn't matter how exhausted my body is either because it's my mind controlling me now. I only sleep when it lets me, which is not very often. It would rather torment me when it can. I usually have my numb switch turned on, but pretending to be alright at school is draining so much out of me. This allows my switch to glitch from time to time, and the emotions I keep away, flood over me and pull me in.

I'm lying here, staring into the darkness like I have for the last few hours, wishing for sleep I know will not come. It's been a long week back at school and I'm glad the term is nearly over. For the two week break, I can stop pretending. I hear my phone vibrate on my bedside table. The light from the screen brightens the room for a few seconds, giving me time to grab it. It's after midnight so I don't know who would be texting me this late. I unlock it and see it's a picture message from JP. Before I can second guess myself, I open it and my breath catches. It's Tamsyn. She's asleep in her bed, curled up on her side with her soft chocolate waves fanning out behind her, cuddling her pillow to her chest. He captioned it, **'Sleepover. The only thing missing is you.'**

My heart pounds out of my chest, my palms get sweaty and tingle. Short, shallow breaths follow and I know it won't be long before I pass out from my panic attack. No matter what I do, she cuts me open. This is why I can't be around her. She makes me feel way more than I'm ready to feel. I miss my girl so much but how can I be her hero when I'm drowning in my own pain? I stare at her sleeping form, wishing I was there holding her in my arms. Knowing I'd rather sink into the darkness by fainting than try and save myself at this point. That's why I'm no good to her now. How can I save her when I'm unwilling to save myself?

Chapter 8

-- Tate --

I've spent all Saturday in bed, ignoring my phone. I couldn't bring myself to delete the picture of Tamsyn, but knowing it is on there is forcing me to avoid my phone. I could stare at her photo all day if I knew it wasn't going to send me into a downward spiral every time I saw it. I'd be lying to myself if I said I didn't miss her. How could I not miss her? She thought I was her lifeline but in reality she was mine. Keeping me above water for as long as she could. I had to let her go and push her away. I don't want to be saved from this darkness. It's what keeps me safe for now. Keeps me safe from the pain I'm not ready to face. How can I face a life without Quinn? My sister. My twin. How does one come to terms with losing a sibling? How am I supposed to live without her? How can I ever feel whole again when my other half is missing? My questions remain unanswered because I'm not ready to face them yet. So I push them aside as they float through my mind, ignoring the pricks of pain associated with them.

My mum knocks on my door before she enters and I see the

sorrow in her eyes, but I choose to ignore it. I can't deal with her pain when I'm using all my energy to keep myself together.

"Tate, why don't you put some sheets on your bed?" she suggests, eyeing the bare mattress. I still haven't replaced the sheets from my sweat inducing nightmare when JP was still here. I ignore the comment and continue to stare at the ceiling. "Do you want to come out to dinner with your dad and I?" she asks, hopeful I might say yes.

"No Mum, I'm fine here," I tell her, not looking her way. I didn't realise it was evening already. I wasted the day away, sitting in the same spot.

"Alright son, we won't be long. Ring me if you need me," she pleads, as she closes the door behind her. Mum and Dad are trying to live as normally as they can after losing Quinn. I think they are doing it for my benefit, trying to get back to some type of normalcy. I don't take much notice of what they do these days. I'm too lost in my own suffering to worry about them.

I know sleep won't come but I don't want to leave my bed. I need to numb the voices in my head. There's only one solution for my problem. Alcohol. I wait until I hear the front door close behind my parents as they leave, then I listen for their car as it starts and drives away. I pull myself from my new favoured spot and drag myself to the liquor cabinet. My parents aren't huge drinkers but at the wake they had a lot of alcohol left over which has now taken up residence in our cabinet. They won't notice if one bottle is missing. I scan the labels to view my choices. I grasp the glass bottle with the brown liquor swimming inside and traipse back to my room. Choosing to sit on the floor and face the door, I grab my phone, switch on a playlist and turn it up as loud as I can. Hoping the mix of loud music and alcohol will drown the voices out.

I don't bother mixing the alcohol, not caring about the burn in my throat as the liquid travels to my belly. Only caring about the reprieve it will eventually give me. I'm a quarter of the way through the bottle when I notice the buzz beginning to take hold. The music changes to Lewis

Capaladi's 'Before you go" and because I'm not ready for it, my heart shatters. The words remind me of Quinn. My heart pounds and I have to gain control of myself before I lose it completely. My breathing steadies after a while as I use my coping strategies to get through. Thoughts of her invade my mind and before I realise it, my feet are leading me to her room.

I haven't set foot in here since she took the pills. My hand shakes as I turn the handle and step through. My breath catches because it's exactly as I remember. It's as immaculate as it always was, with nothing out of place. Her bright orange feature wall on one side with the off white paint covering the rest of the room. Another thing to add to her list of quirky things she did. Her dresser against the opposite wall has photos stuck into the frame, to hold them in place. There's a few of her with Avery and Monique but it's the one of me and her when we were kids which catches my eye. We are dressed up in halloween costumes. We must be about nine or ten. She wanted to go as Cinderella and made Mum dress me up as her Prince Charming. I told her she couldn't marry me as I was her brother. She said I was her real life Prince, always watching over her and protecting her, so it didn't matter to her. Why did she have so much faith in me? Why couldn't I have protected her like she believed I could?

I place the photo in my pocket, wanting to keep it for myself. Hoping she still saw me as her prince after all this time. My eye catches the pink polka dotted book sitting unopened on her dresser. She was always carrying this journal around with her and would get crazy if anyone touched it. She's not here to get mad now so I hesitantly pick it up and flick through the pages. A splash of red paint has me stopping and opening up to the page. It's as if she's guided me to this page, to satisfy a question I never thought I'd get an answer to.

She wrote: *I've seen Tate roll his eyes at my suggestion for a red door but I want it badly. It will bring some positive energy my way I desperately need. A red door has a few meanings I've found. The ones I connect with the most are the fact it signifies a safe place to rest as well as positive and welcoming energy. My greatest reason for the red door though is because it provides protection. Will it protect me from my own mind, I wonder.*

This was dated years ago. Was she plagued for this many years with problems she couldn't handle on her own? How could I not see it? How did I not see she wasn't coping? She needed me but I was so absorbed in my own life, I didn't see how hers was going. I flick slower through the pages and stop at a poem which catches my eye. Under the title is her name. Did she write this?

Trapped by Darkness

By Quinn Devereaux

The world sees my shell

But I'm hidden inside

Quiet and shy

Screaming tears that have dried

Voices get louder

And drown out my soul

Until what is left

Is nowhere near whole

I'm tired and numb

From the pain of my voices

I've let them take over

They dictate my choices

Cutting me deep

Where nobody sees

Cursing, defeating

They're so hard to please

 Darkness takes over

There's no end in sight

Consumed by these thoughts

That block out the light

 They're killing me slowly

I'm losing the battle

Knives cutting me deeper

I feel like a hassle

 Wanting to sleep

And rewind back the clock

To a happier me

Without a padlock

 Trapped in the darkness

With these unshed tears

Only kept company

By what feasts on my fears

 Tortured and chained

When will it all end

I'm tired and lonely

Don't want to pretend

   Why can't the world see

Screams for help behind eyes

That say I'm okay

And other hurtful lies

   Caged in this prison

Is a broken me

That wonders how much longer

I can fight to be free

Her words eerily speak to me. It's as if she's read my mind in advance and projected my thoughts onto the page. This is exactly how I feel at times. Was she drowning in the same darkness I now use as a comfort to keep me safe? Was it the world or the darkness she was wanting so badly to escape from? These questions plague my mind and frustrate me because I know I will never get the chance to know the answers.

Chapter 9

-- Tamsyn --

It's Friday, our last day of term one and we are enjoying our lunch outside in the sun. Penny has decided to join our group at lunch-times now. She would usually sit with whoever she saw first after she grabbed her tray. I'm hoping she has found a permanent home with us because she fits in perfectly. I have caught her and JP sneaking glances at each other when they think no one is looking. She usually blushes from embarrassment after being caught. JP on the other hand, shrugs like it's no big deal he got caught checking her out.

"Has everyone decided what they are picking for their skills and life lesson classes?" Scott asks around a mouthful of food. I forgot I was supposed to talk to Penny about her choices.

I turn to her and ask, "Penny, did you want to do the self-defence classes with me?"

Her eyes light up as she replies, "Yes. I was thinking of taking self-defence. It'll be more fun if we do it together."

"Yay. That's one class sorted then. How many do we have to choose?" I say to no one in particular.

"I think you pick three because first aid is compulsory. So in total, we have four new classes," Scott says.

" I should do the driving lessons. It's about time I learnt how to drive," I say with my head hanging low. My dad was supposed to teach me how to drive.

"Nah, we can teach you how to drive. Can't we guys?" JP says, and there are nods all around the table.

I lift my head and with tears shining in my eyes I ask, "Are you guys sure you have the patience for it?" I'm wondering if I might be better off with a professional driving tutor.

"Yeah, it'll be fun T," Scott says, not bringing attention to the fact I'm on the verge of crying.

"Okay, if you guys insist," I say. "That still leaves me with two classes to choose."

"What about the Pasta from scratch class? Then you could cook me pasta every day. My mouth is watering just thinking about it," Rafe says, as he daydreams about filling his stomach.

"Umm no thanks. Maybe you should take it then you can cook for yourself like a grown up," I say, trying not to laugh. He always knows what to say to cheer me up.

"I can't. I've already decided to pick the observatory trip with the guys. You need to pick one in the section for day trips. There's pasta from scratch class, observatory, fishing, or helping out at the animal shelter. We're all stuck doing first aid then I've picked mechanics where you learn the ins and outs of a car. For my last choice I chose power tools so I can be a man around the house for the ladies," he says proudly.

"Is that what you guys are taking too?" I ask JP and Scott.

"Yeah, those are the ones I'm taking," JP says. Of course he would take the same classes as his best friend.

"I'm going to the observatory because it was my idea. I get sea sick so fishing was out. Like everyone I've gotta do first aid and I'm doing the car mechanics course. I've chosen building an online blog instead of power tools. Thought it might be a good skill to have in our modern world," Scott says.

"Ugh I don't want to do any of those. What else is there?" I ask.

"What about Tots and Toddlers? People bring in their babies and toddlers and you learn how to care for them?" Rafe says.

"Why would I want to learn how to look after babies? You have to have sex to have babies and I haven't been doing any of that," I say before I can censor myself, causing Rafe to spit his food all over the table. "Eww Rafe," I say, wrinkling my nose as the table goes quiet and they all turn to stare at me.

"You have had sex at least once though, haven't you?" Rafe asks, and I notice they are all waiting for my answer.

My cheeks heat and I reply while looking at the table, "No I haven't. I'm a virgin."

"Not even with Blake? You were with him for so long," Penny jumps into the conversation as curious as the guys.

"Nope. That's probably why he started sleeping with Leyla because I kept avoiding his advances. It never felt right with him," I say, and Penny nods. However the guys look at me as if I've grown three heads.

"I don't think I could have gone this long being a virgin," Rafe pipes in, and Scott and JP nod along with him agreeing. "In fact I don't know any guy our age who is still a virgin," he adds.

"Lucky I'm not a guy then, isn't it?" I say, wishing this conversation never came up.

A light goes on behind JP's eyes and he says, "I know one guy who is still a virgin and he is pretty proud of the fact too. He doesn't try to hide it or anything."

"Who?" Rafe and Scott nosily ask together.

"He who must not be named," JP says smugly.

Rafe scratches his head and with a confused look on his face asks, "Voldemort?"

"No, you idiot. Tate," JP says, looking right at me with a smirk on his face. From his revelation, I know my face is slowly turning the shade of a ripe tomato. Tate's a virgin too. The bell for the end of lunch goes and I'm lost in my thoughts and no closer to having my life skills classes picked.

I'm sitting in human bio at the end of the day and the conversation at lunch time has me missing Tate. I never would have thought he was a virgin. He was always so confident and sure of himself. I guess you can't judge a book by it's cover.

"T," Scott says, as he nudges me in the arm and breaks me from my thoughts. I turn my gaze away from the empty seat next to me and take the piece of paper he's handing me. Ms. Chadwick has been talking but I've been in a trance staring at Tate's old chair. I didn't hear a word she said.

"What's this?" I ask Scott, as I look over what's printed on it.

"You need to put your name on the top and tick the three skills and life lesson classes you want to do. Pick one from the day trip and then two others from the main list. Don't worry about first aid as everyone's doing it," he informs me.

"Damn it. I still haven't decided," I say, as I read the list. I come across the self-defence class in my scanning so I tick that. Now what else can I choose? Nothing else interests me and since the guys are going to teach me to drive, that's out. I spot a sewing class so tick that as it might come in handy with fixing up all my baggy clothes. I haven't been able to gain any of the weight I've lost. I haven't regained much of an appetite which hasn't helped. I never got around to asking Penny what other classes she was going to choose so I can't copy her.

"You should pick the observatory trip. It'll be fun if we all do it together. Penny too. Quickly send her a text while Ms. Chadwick is distracted," Scott tells me. It does sound like it wouldn't be too bad if we all went. I hurriedly pull out my phone from my bag and send a text to Penny.

Tamsyn: Hey pick observatory if you can, Scott talked me into it

My phone vibrates practically straight away with a reply.

Penny: Was texting you the same thing as JP talked me into it

Tamsyn: Do you think they planned this?

Penny: Who cares? At least it'll be fun and we will all be together :)

Tamsyn: Stars are pretty great

Penny: True plus fish guts would freak me out

I quickly put my phone away as Ms. Chadwick comes around, collecting the forms. I tick the observatory and feel satisfied with my choices. Self-defence will protect me, sewing will help clothe me and the observatory will help me to remember to shine. I only wish my green-eyed boy was going to be there with me. I think he needs the reminder more than me.

"Me and Penny are coming to the observatory," I tell Rafe and Scott with a wide smile and they grin back at me.

"Yay. I'm happy you guys are coming but I was looking forward to eating all the pasta you could have made me," Rafe says, and his face drops with his lips popping out in a pout.

"Always thinking about your stomach," I say giggling. I hand Ms. Chadwick my form as she passes our table and I can't help but glance to Tate's chair and wonder what he would have chosen, if he was still here.

Chapter 10
~

-- Tamsyn --

Lately I've been feeling lighter. The black cloud usually following me around is smaller and further away than usual. The waves crashing over me only come every so often instead of constantly. The guys and Penny have a lot to do with it. The holidays have gone by fast, with my friends making them more enjoyable than I ever thought they would be. We've had a lot of sleepovers at my place over the break with the guys choosing to spend more nights in than out at parties. We did have a smaller party at Penny's last weekend but it wasn't anywhere near as crowded as usual. We spent a lot of days out at the mall and went to the movies a couple of times too.

They've done their best to keep me distracted but today I've ended up down at the dock, thinking of Dad. It's completely different in the light of day. At night the buildings across the bay twinkle like stars but standing there in the sunshine, I can almost pretend Dad has jumped into the water and will surface at any second. He'd always hold his breath and swim under the surface for a ridiculous amount of time. Closing my eyes I can remember his voice calling me into the water. A hand touches my shoulder and the spell is broken. Twisting around I spot Rafe, all large and real.

"Hey Petal, you okay? I was out for a run and noticed you," he says, concern dripping from his voice. It's like a wave leaps out of the bay and hits me. I'm gasping for breath and sobbing because it should be my beautiful boy out here for his run. Why doesn't Tate need me as much as I need him? I cry an embarrassing amount into Rafe's chest and he holds me in silence while I let out the pain. When I've composed myself again, he walks me home like today was normal, just two friends out for a walk.

I joke and ask, "You haven't put a tracking device on my phone have you?" It's the second time he has rescued me from the dock.

His laugh fills the air as he tells me, "It's my 'damsel in distress' radar. The ladies love a knight in shining armour so I gotta stay in practice." His response makes me laugh along with him. We walk the rest of the way in silence. He doesn't breathe a word about my breakdown as he walks me to my door. We act as if it didn't happen.

"Bye Tamsyn," he says, giving me one of his bright smiles before he jogs away from me, continuing on with his run. I spend the rest of my day in bed indulging in memories of my dad and of Tate. It's only a few days until school starts back so I make a deal with myself. I'll give myself today to let it all wash over me then like a wave, I'll let it flow back out to sea where it'll stay before it crashes back over me. Even though the waves have started to space themselves further apart, the hurt is still as raw as ever when they do arrive.

The rest of the weekend flies by and now it's the first day back at school since the holidays. They've changed everyone's schedules so we can fit in our life lesson classes. Everyone in the senior year level has to meet in the school hall this morning so that's where me and the guys find Penny. We have to collect our schedules. I'm hoping I have at least one of them in my first aid class since we all have to do it. I search through the containers marked W for my last name and pull out my new schedule. So for this term, it shows every Wednesday first period I have first aid, Thursday first period I have sewing and Thursday last period I have self-defence. Taking my schedule, I huddle with Penny and the guys.

"Okay, who has first aid on Wednesday during first period?" I ask them, as they all scan over the papers in their hands.

"I do," Rafe and JP pipe up, and I hold up my hand for a high five which they both deliver.

"I've got Wednesday second period," Penny says, a lot less enthusiastic.

"Ooh me too Penny," Scott says, smiling at her and she returns it.

"Awesome," she says, looking at him and I can't help but look at JP and see his face drop. I bet he hoped he would be in the same class as Penny.

"Sucks we aren't together for first aid but we're both in self-defence, yeah?" I ask Penny, and she nods.

"I didn't know what else to choose so left it blank. By the looks of it, they've put me in sewing on Thursday mornings," she says, and I get filled with excitement.

"Yay, you are with me because I picked the sewing class," I tell her and we laugh together, excited we have more classes together.

"When do we go to the observatory? It doesn't say," Rafe says, turning his paper over to inspect the back in case he missed something.

"I think they organise a day for later in the term and we do a day trip," Scott informs us.

"Cool. Hope it's a school day. Anything beats being in the classroom," Rafe says.

"Students, if you'd like to take your seats. I'll quickly talk to you about this term and then you can be on your way," Principal Astle says. We all shuffle into a row and sit down. "Welcome back. By now you should have your new schedules in your hands. You will see first aid is compulsory and we've split you up into groups which you will stay in for the duration of the term. Next, if you didn't tick enough boxes when we handed out the options, we have slotted you into a class which has free space. Hopefully it is a skill that will benefit you in the future, or at the very least you enjoy learning. And lastly with regards to the field trip options. We will be scheduling those for a Saturday in the middle of the term. We will update you further when we have organised everything. I'm glad to see you all back in high spirits. I hope it continues throughout the term. Period one is still going so you can go to your classes now. Enjoy your first day back everyone," he says, as he walks away from the microphone dismissing us.

We all say our goodbyes and walk off in different directions. I walk with Penny and Scott to English. At least the term is starting on a high note. Let's hope it continues.

Wednesday morning rolls around quite fast. Since school started back, I feel like the week has flown by. Today we have our first aid class so Jp, Rafe and I walk together to the hall to get started. As we enter, there are about twenty other kids in the class with us. Two paramedics stand in the centre of the hall, surrounded by all sorts of equipment. I didn't realise they were getting proper professionals to do these lessons.

"What are your names?" The lady paramedic asks us, as she holds up what I'm guessing is a roll.

"I'm Rafe, this is JP and this is Tamsyn," Rafe says, pointing at us.

"Hi, I'm Lily and this is my partner Zac. We are your instructors for the term," she says, and then scrolls the list for our names. Her brows pinch in the middle of her forehead before she says, "JP, is that short for something? I don't have a JP on the list."

"John Peterson," he tells her, and she smiles.

"Yes, that's here. Do you prefer JP?" she asks, looking at him.

"Yes please," he says, politely.

"Not a problem. I'll make a note here to call you JP."

"Thanks," JP says, and we leave her to join the circle with the rest of the students.

"We should call you JPP instead, John Paul Peterson," Rafe says, trying to rile JP. For his efforts, JP swats him on the back of the head.

"Don't be a dick," JP says, with a smile. He never takes anything Rafe says to heart so they are laughing about it within moments.

"Okay class so I'll introduce ourselves again. I'm Lily and this is Zac and we are both paramedics. I've been one for six years and Zac for five years," Lily starts, and we all listen carefully.

"Now we want everyone to take this class seriously but still have fun. Remember, everything you learn in this class could help you to potentially save a life one day," she says, looking around the room at each of us individually to make sure we are listening. "Today, we are going to learn what to do if someone is bleeding heavily from a wound or if someone has been burnt. Let's get started."

Zac walks around handing out first aid sheets to everyone. They do a demonstration to show us all what to do if we encounter someone injured and bleeding. We can also use the same techniques if we injure ourselves and are bleeding. We split off into smaller groups. I stay with JP and Rafe and we work together to bandage up imaginary wounds on each other. Rafe keeps flustering me as he jokes about bleeding out because I'm not fast enough to patch up his wound. After some time working on bleeding wounds, we move onto burns and they do the same thing. Zac and Lily explain and do a demonstration. We work together through pretend scenarios and figure out what we would do if faced with a burn victim. Walking out of the class, I'm excited for next week's lesson. It went so fast and was quite enjoyable. It was definitely not what I was expecting.

Chapter 11

-- Tate --

The school holidays were a blur. I didn't leave the house once, content to stay in my room, absorbed in my thoughts. My parents tried numerous times to get me to do something with them but I declined every invitation. Same with Pierce and Xander. They invited me to a few parties but I didn't want to socialise with anyone. The darkness inside me was the only company I could handle. They didn't force the issue, letting me know they were there for me if I needed them. Mum quickly put sheets on my bed when I dragged myself to the shower one day. It honestly hadn't crossed my mind to do it myself. It didn't seem important enough to bother myself with.

Since I've found Quinn's journal it's like I've been walking around in a dream. I can see everyone around me at school and they're talking to me, but I'm disconnected. It's as if my body is there but my mind is on a different plane. I think my brain is seeking refuge again. It doesn't want to get sucked into another void of sorrow bought on by Quinn's journal. I haven't dared open it up again. I'm too scared. I have no clue what I might find. Is this what she felt like before she took those pills? I wonder if the darkness she feared is the same one I use as a comfort to keep me safe from pain. I can leave the darkness whenever I want though, can't I? She said she couldn't escape it. It's not the same as mine, is it? I'll stay numb a bit longer. I'm not ready to confront the pain yet. I doubt I will ever be ready. Maybe that's the problem.

I zone back in to what's going on around me and catch Pierce and Xander mid conversation.

"Yeah it's going to be a big one I heard," Xander says.

"What's this?" I ask.

"Jax is having a party tonight for his eighteenth birthday. We were thinking we should go. Most of our senior year will be there. You in?" Pierce asks. I stare at my two best friends, studying them and see the hope in their faces. I haven't been the best friend lately so why not. It's just a party. I'm positive I can handle a party.

"Sure, I'm in," I say.

"Yes," they both say, and then high five each other. I feel dumb asking but I've been in a bubble all week and I don't know what day it is.

"Is it Friday today?" I ask, hoping they won't notice I'm losing track of my days.

"Yeah man, it is," Pierce says, giving me a sad smile. He pats me on the back as he turns his attention to Xander so they can organise the night. I force myself to keep focussed. Jax's house isn't too far from Pierce's so we are going to walk over so we can all drink instead of needing a sober driver. Works for me. I could do with a night of numbing my mind.

When I arrive home after school, I tell Mum I'm going to a party with Pierce and Xander. Her excitement levels are way higher than mine at this point. I assume it's because I'm doing something other than lying in bed, staring at the ceiling. I jump in the shower and while alone, I take a few moments to myself. I blast the heat on my skin and stand under it, eyes closed, focussing on my breathing. Repeating my mantra, don't think over and over, I zone out and welcome the peace I feel for a minute.

I shake myself out of my bereft state, turn the shower off and step out. I wipe my hand over the fogged up mirror and stare at the shell of myself. Where did the Tate I know go? The guy I'm looking at needs a haircut. The faded purple tinge under my eyes signifies my inability to sleep. I use my towel to dry myself off and wrap it around me, before going back to my room. I throw on the first clothes I find, not caring what I wear. It happens to be a white t-shirt and jeans. I sit on the side of the bed and catch a glimpse of Quinn's journal sticking out from where I stowed it under my pillow. All of a sudden, the room feels smaller. I need to get out of here. I snatch my phone off the dresser and hurry from my room.

"I'll see you later Mum, might crash at Pierce's if it's late," I yell on my way out of the big red door. Everytime I see my front door, I am reminded of Quinn. She's everywhere and nowhere at the same time. I shake my head to ease my thoughts of her but it doesn't work. Why now? Damn it. I need to run. It's worked in the past. My feet pick up speed and I let my feet pound the pavement, all the way to Pierce's.

I open his door when I arrive, not knocking as I know he will be home getting ready for the party. What friend knocks on their best friend's door these days anyway?

"Pierce?" I yell out, as I close the door behind me. He comes out of his kitchen with raised brows and a sandwich in his hands.

"Hey man, I didn't think I'd see you until a bit later." He looks me up and down noticing I'm breathing hard with a light sweat covering my face. "Did you run all the way here?" I nod, and he pops back into the kitchen and comes back with a bottle of water. "Here, it looks like you need this," he says, handing it to me. I unscrew the cap and guzzle down half of it before I replace the lid.

"Thanks man," I say.

"Is everything alright?" he asks, as he takes a bite of his sandwich.

"Yeah man. I'm fine. I just wanted to get out of the house," I say, still huffing from my run. He looks unconvinced but doesn't push me to talk, which I appreciate.

"You hungry?" he asks, gesturing to his sandwich. "I can make you one."

I shake my head and say, "Nah man, I'm good."

"Come, let's go to my room. I'll put on some music while I get ready. I'm sure Xander won't be too far away," he says, leading me down the hall to his room.

"Are your parents still at work?" I ask, as his house is quiet.

"Yeah, they've got some fundraiser they're going to tonight. Makenna is staying at her boyfriend's house for the weekend. She's hardly ever home these days anyway with college and work," he explains. I haven't seen his older sister since I left to go stay with JP.

"I grabbed some bottles of bourbon on my way home if you want to get started. There's some Coca-Cola in the fridge for mixing. Make us some drinks and I'll jump in the shower," he says. He turned eighteen a couple months ago so he can legally buy alcohol now, making it easier for when we want to drink.

"Sweet man, where's the bourbon?" I ask. He opens his wardrobe door and pulls out two glass bottles. He sets one on his dresser and hands the other to me. I take it with me as I walk back through the house to the kitchen. I practically lived at this house growing up so I know where everything is. I grab three glasses out of the cupboard, making a drink for Xander too. I know Xander and he always arrives earlier than expected when there's a party happening. I fish some ice out of the freezer, grab the fizzy drink from the fridge and mix the drinks. I add a bit more bourbon to mine and a lot less Coca-Cola. I swallow a mouthful down, throw my head back and close my eyes. Don't think. Don't think.

Don't think I tell myself. Am I ever going to be able to survive without my mantra?

The squeaking of the front door has me coming back to reality. I pop my head around the corner to see Xander closing the door.

"Hey Xan, got a drink ready for you in here," I call over to him. He turns towards my voice and smiles.

"You been here long?" he asks, as he enters the kitchen and picks up one of the full glasses, taking a sip.

"Not long. Pierce is in the shower," I say, taking a sip of my own. He takes a seat on a bar stool, on the other side of the kitchen bench.

"I hope there's some hot, single girls there tonight. I'm in the mood for some loving," he says, smiling so wide his dimples show.

"I'm sure there will be plenty of girls for you to love on," I say, trying not to laugh. This is what I need, time with my friends. Tonight will be a good distraction from my life.

"You're always in the mood for some loving. What's new?" I hear Pierce say from behind me, mocking Xander.

"You two can be my wing men," Xander says, looking hopeful at me and Pierce.

"Not me man, I'm on a drinking buzz tonight," I say, and they both laugh.

"You are always on a drinking buzz. When are you gonna be on a girl buzz?" Xander asks, and I roll my eyes at him.

"When a green fairy comes along," Pierce says, and they both crack up laughing.

Since we have the house to ourselves, we sit around and have a few more drinks before we make our way to Jax's house. It is a few streets away and it's not long before we can hear the music, blasting from his house.

"It sounds like one heck of a party," Xander says with excitement. The closer we get, the louder the music becomes. There are people in the front yard drinking so we navigate our way through the side fence and head around to the back. Jax lives in a large two storey house with a huge back yard. It's the perfect set up for a party. A lot of the people we see are from school. I've grown up with most of them so I'm hoping none of them come up to me in their drunken states. I want to forget tonight and if people pester me, I know I will get irritated.

There's a table set up against the house with different alcohol and mixes. There's a keg of beer next to it, where people can fill their cups from. Pierce steps over to the table, grabs three cups and hands them out to me and Xander.

He pours us a shot size amount of bourbon in each and says, "Shots up," and we drink them down. The more I drink lately, the easier it is to handle the burn at the start of the night. I know it won't be long before I don't feel the burn or much of anything.

"Do you guys want to go inside or hang out here?" Xander asks.

"I'm not fussed," I say.

"Let's stay here for a minute and see what everyone is doing before we decide?" Pierce suggests, as he pours another shot into our cups.

Several shots later and I'm feeling the buzz. Me and the guys are laughing about the time Pierce tried to do a trick shot on his skateboard over a pole. He ended up with road rash down one side of his body and had to go to the emergency department. They had to pick out all the debris and clean out his injuries. It was not a pretty sight. It's funny looking back at it now, but his parents didn't think it was funny at the time. We got banned from his place for two whole weeks, which felt like a lifetime when we were thirteen.

We finally decide to roam and check out the inside of the house. I haven't eaten anything since lunch time so the alcohol is hitting me hard, making me stumble over my feet as I follow the guys. There's more people in here and everyone is squished together, yelling over the roaring music to be heard. We bump into Jax as we are hunting around for somewhere to park ourselves for the night.

"Happy birthday man," I say, as I give him a one armed hug.

"Thanks Tate. Sorry I haven't talked to you since Quinn. I didn't know what to say, you know." He brings up the person who I'm trying to drown out.

"It's okay," I say, as I quickly walk away from him. I can't stand there any longer because I don't want to break down in the middle of a party. I see a couch being vacated so I hurry to it, tugging on Pierce's shirt to get his attention so he follows. He grabs Xander and we all squeeze onto the small space. I stick my cup out in Pierce's direction and on cue, he pours me another shot.

"I might grab a mix to go with this. I don't think I can keep up with the shots," Xander says, as he hops up from the couch to go off on his search.

"He's going to hunt for girls," Pierce yells at me, and we both laugh knowing it's exactly what he's doing. Pierce happily sits with me, shooting back the bourbon. Other friends of ours come over and make conversation but then head off when they see a familiar face in the crowd. I haven't been to a party this packed in a long time.

"I need to piss," I say to Pierce.

"I'll stay here and hold the couch," he says, so I gulp down the drink in my cup and stand. The alcohol swimming in my veins has made me numb, exactly what I wanted. I stumble through the crowd of people and line up outside the toilet, behind a few other people and wait my turn. I lean my head against the wall and close my eyes for a second.

"Your turn Tate," someone says, as I'm poked in the arm. My eyes take a second to adjust and I see it's Monique, Quinn's friend.

"Thanks Mon," I say, stumbling into the toilet, busting to go and needing to get away from her. I feel better after relieving myself. I try to act more sober than I am when leaving the bathroom but I end up needing the wall to hold me up. I'm getting tired so I decide to lean my head against the wall for a moment and rest. The blaring music disappears and quiet follows. I feel a tug of my hand and then I'm being pushed back onto a bed. This is what I need. I need to sleep. The alcohol has truly taken over now.

There's a weight on my lap and then I hear, "Tate," whispered into my ear.

"Sweetness?" I say, through the haze. Is she here?

"Yeah, it's me baby." She lifts my floppy hands and places them on her waist but something in the back of my mind registers something is wrong. Whoever this body belongs to, it's wrong. I peel my heavy eyes open to see brown eyes staring at me.

"Eyes aren't blue," I slur, and her hyena laugh pierces my ears.

"Of course they're not silly," she says, and I instantly recognise Avery's voice.

"Get off me. What are you doing?" I yell, as I push her off me. I stagger to my feet and turn to look at her. She's standing in her bra with her skirt pushed up her thighs, holding her phone in one hand.

"I know you want me Tate. Just give in to me already," she says, walking towards me.

"I don't want you. Leave me alone Avery," I say, as I back up to the door and fling it open. I stumble into the hallway and see Pierce up ahead.

"Tate. Where have you been, man? I've been looking for you," he says, as he grabs my arm.

"She's a bloody psycho. Keep her away from me. I gotta go." I rush out and push my way past people to find my way outside. As soon as I get outside, I bend over a bush and the disgust ejects from my stomach, taking away all the loathing I have inside as well as any moments that happen after it.

-- Tamsyn --

"Huh?" I say, into the darkness. What is that noise? I wake up and realise it's my phone ringing. I awkwardly grab the phone and swipe to answer it, without looking at who is calling. It must be important if they are ringing in the middle of the night. "Hello?" I say, sitting up in the darkness and leaning back against the wall. For a second I don't hear anything but then my ears pick up a sniffling, on the other end of the line. "Hello? Are you there?" I ask again, and this time I can hear a distinct whimpering, their pain echoes through the phone. I pull the phone away from my ear and glance to see the name on the screen. My heart misses a beat as I read 'Tate.' I sit up, pulling my knees to my chest and rest my chin on them.

"Tate?" I say into the phone, hoping he will talk so I can hear the voice I've missed terribly. All I can hear are his cries of pain. Is he hurt? "Tate, are you okay?" I beg, but he doesn't say anything. "Please talk to me," I plead, not sure if he can hear me at all.

"Why did she have to leave me?" he yells, and my heart cracks at the anguish in his voice. "Why did she have to leave me behind?" he cries out. I don't know what to say so I stay silent, letting him release all his pain. "How am I supposed to live without her? I don't want to live without her," he screams. I've never heard him in so much pain. "I didn't get to say goodbye. I just want to say goodbye. How could she do this to me? She selfishly left me here to suffer. I don't want to be here without her." My own tears fall freely as the boy I need, desperately grieves openly for his sister. I remain silent, I don't know if he knows I'm here.

"Quinny, I'm sorry I couldn't protect you from yourself. I'm not much of a prince after all, am I? Why did you have to take yourself away from me? Why couldn't you stay? I need you back Quinny. Please come back," he rambles on talking to her as if she's there with him. Prickling worry creeps up my neck.

"Tate, where are you?" I ask him, with tears welling up in my eyes.

"I'm with Quinn," he says sadly, and my heart gallops in my chest. I hope he isn't doing anything stupid.

"Where are you and Quinn?" I ask, hoping he will give me a straight answer. I think he's drunk, with the way he is talking in circles.

"I'm visiting her. I needed to see her," he says, sniffling. He must be at her grave. I hope he's there. He sounds like he's alone and drunk. I don't think he's in a good state so I put him on speaker while I open my messages and text JP, hoping he's awake and will get my message.

Tamsyn: Please be awake JP. Tate is on the phone. I think he's at Quinn's grave and he's drunk. Sounds in a bad way. Can you contact someone to get him please? I'm worried

My text must wake JP up, as it takes over a minute for his reply to come through.

JP: I'm on it. Don't stress

I keep Tate on speaker in case JP texts again. I sit there in the dark and listen to his soft cries, wanting nothing more than to hold him in my arms but I'm not able to. My heart breaks with his pain. I sit there, listening to his breathing between his whimpers for about ten minutes, before I can't take it anymore.

"Tate?" I softly say, trying to reach him.

I hear a sharp intake of breath before he says, "Sweetness?" and my heart melts at the use of my nickname. I didn't realise how much that name meant to me until now.

"I'm here Tate. I'm here," I say, not knowing what else to do. I know no words will console his pain. When my dad died, there wasn't anything anyone said to make the pain hurt less. I only ever wanted someone to be there with me, to sit by me while I suffered with my pain. But no one did. I had to do it alone. His cries grow louder as he lets out all the hurt and pain he's been keeping inside. I hurt right alongside him.

"Why did she leave me?" he cries out, in a soul wrenching scream.

"I don't know Tate. I don't know," I reply between sobs, knowing nothing I say will heal his pain right now.

"I just want her back," he cries to me.

"I know Tate," I sadly say, knowing exactly how he feels. All I ever wanted when my dad died, was for him to come back. I would've given anything for him to come back.

Lost in my own thoughts, I nearly miss him saying, "I'm sorry Sweetness."

"You don't need to be sorry. It's okay," I say, hoping I can comfort him.

Then he says, "No, you don't understand. I'm sorry I can't love you in the darkness." My soul breaks for my broken boy. He's completely lost himself in his grief.

"You don't need to worry Tate, I will hold the torch and show you the way out," I say, wiping the tears from my wet face. I hear his breathing pick up as his cries increase. I know by the way he can't catch his breath, a panic attack is starting. Have I triggered him again?

"Tate?" I yell into the phone, and I hear an echo on the other end.

I listen and hear a guy say, "Shit. Tate? It's okay. Calm down, breathe man, breathe. Look at me. That's it. In and out. In and out. I got you brother. Just breathe. I got you." I listen to the kind voice on the other end of the phone with Tate and know he's in good hands. Tate's breathing slows down and the panic attack subsides.

"I miss them so much," I hear Tate cry to the mystery guy with the kind voice.

"Them?" the mystery guy questions. I hear Tate mumble but can't make out what he says.

"Let's get you home man," the kind voice says, and I hear him grunting. "Xander, hurry up. I need you," he yells out.

I hear puffing and then another voice says, "Sorry but you're too fast. You took off like Superman and I couldn't keep up. Ugh I shouldn't have drunk so much. I think I might vomit."

"Help me get him to his feet," the kind voice says, and they both grunt and curse as they help Tate up. '

"Sweetness?" I hear Tate say, but his voice is far away. I don't think his phone is by his ear anymore.

"What's Sweetness?" the puffing voice asks.

"I think he was on the phone," the kind voice says, and I hear his voice clearer. He must have picked up Tate's phone. "Hello?"

"Hi. I'm Tamsyn but Tate calls me Sweetness," I say to the kind stranger, blushing in the dark at having to explain my nickname.

"Well hello Tamsyn aka Sweetness, it's nice to meet you," he says, and I can hear the smile in his voice.

"Did JP send you?" I ask.

"Yeah, he did. How did you know?" he asks, his voice laced with curiosity.

"Tate rang me and was acting and talking really weird so I texted JP to send help," I explain.

"Well, thanks for that. I was worried when he took off and I couldn't find him. It's good to know he has an angel on his side," he says softly.

I hear Tate in the background mumbling, "Green fairy. She's my green fairy."

"No way. The green fairy exists. This is unbelievable. Let me talk to her?" the puffing voice says excitedly. Then someone must cover the phone with their hand because I can hear voices but they sound buried under water. I can't make out what they are saying.

"Sorry about that Tamsyn. Don't worry, we will get Tate home safely," he says.

"Thanks. Ah I don't know your name?" I say, wanting a name to put to the voice.

"Oh sorry it's been a long night. I'm Pierce and the slow poke here is Xander. We are Tate's best friends." Best friends? Hearing that hurts because Tate had been calling me his best friend.

Before I can say anything I hear Tate ramble, "She's my best friend too. She's part of them," and with only a few words, he stitches a piece of my heart back into place.

"Well, Tate's other best friend, what I think he's trying to say is that he misses you. I better go so we can lug him home. You going to be okay?" Pierce asks.

"Yeah, I will be now. Thanks. Bye," I say.

"Bye Tamsyn," Pierce says, before he disconnects the call and I take a deep breath, grateful they are there to get him home safely. I remember JP and quickly send him a text.

Tamsyn: Thanks JP. His friends Pierce and Xander got him and are taking him home.

JP: Glad to hear that. I knew they would find him. Are you ok?

Tamsyn: Yeah. Just glad he's safe. I better get some sleep. Night JP

JP: Night Ice Queen x

I put my phone down and snuggle back under my covers, hugging my pillow to my chest. The adrenaline from hearing his voice pulses through me, causing me to feel wide awake. Is Pierce right? Did Tate mean it? Does he miss me? I focus on my breathing and think of ways I can help him to heal. I won't let sober him stop me. I have to try. It's with thoughts of Tate in my head, I eventually drift off to sleep.

Chapter 12

-- Tate --

I wake up with my head throbbing and can hear hushed voices coming from behind me. I keep my eyes closed for a moment as I rub a hand down my face. I massage my temples, hoping it will help the killer headache I can feel coming on. When I finally open my eyes, the bright light makes it hurt more but my eyes soon adjust. I notice my surroundings and realise I've slept on Pierce's couch but I have no recollection of how I got here. The voices are still talking, so I push myself up to stand and follow the direction they are coming from. They lead me to the kitchen, where I find Pierce and Xander seated on bar stools, sipping on coffee. They both turn my way when they hear my heavy footsteps.

"You're awake. Do you want a coffee? I just boiled the kettle," Pierce says, and I nod, not ready to use words. I grab a mug, make a black coffee and add some cold water from the tap, needing the caffeine hit straight away to sober me up. I gulp down a big mouthful and it makes my queasy stomach gurgle. I hope it doesn't come back up. That makes the memory of me vomiting in the bush pop into my head.

"Ugh, did I vomit in the bushes last night?" I ask, as I look at my two best friends, hoping they can fill in the gaps. They glance at each other and shrug.

"I'm not sure. You might have done when you took off," Xander says, as he takes a sip of his coffee.

"I took off?" I ask, not remembering.

"Do you remember anything from last night?" Pierce asks. I search my brain for memories and say them out loud so the guys can help me with the timeline.

"I remember arriving at the party. We hung out in the backyard for a bit before we went in and bumped into Jax." As I'm talking they're nodding, so I keep trying to recall the memories through the haze. "Xander, you took off once we were inside and it gets a bit blurry after that," I say, as I gulp down another mouthful, hoping the caffeine will help with my memory.

"Do you remember Avery?" Pierce asks, peeking at me. I stare at him thinking, trying to catch a memory with her and I only get a glimpse.

"I remember her in a room, with a bra on. Oh my God. I didn't do anything with her, did I?" I say, worrying something happened with Avery. I can't stand her now.

"No, I don't think you did. From what Monique told me, you were practically passed out standing up. Avery dragged you to the closest room and tried to seduce you. The next thing I know you were stumbling out of a room, screaming at me to keep psycho Avery away from you. You drew quite a few stares from people," he says. I'm in shock because I can't place the memory anywhere. Most of my night is blank.

He takes a sip of his own drink and continues on, "Avery didn't help the situation by walking out of the room in her bra. She made it look like something definitely went on between you two. I'd expect rumours to be circulating already," he says, like me getting accused of hooking up with Avery isn't a big deal. It is to me. "Do you remember anything else? Anything at all?" he asks, and I see a twinkle in his eye. He knows something and he's waiting for me to have an aha moment where I remember. My mind is completely blank so I don't think it's going to happen.

"I can't remember anything else," I say again, looking between them hoping they will give me answers about what went on.

"I can't hold it in any more. You've been holding out on us man," Xander says, practically bouncing on his stool with glee.

"What are you talking about?" I'm concerned about whatever has him so excited. The look on his face changes and now he looks like a kid on Christmas morning who is about to open their presents.

"The green fairy. She does exist," he shouts at me, and my heart drops. I told them about Tamsyn. "See! There's guilt written all over your face. You deliberately kept her from us," Xander says, happily.

"What did I tell you about her?" I ask sadly, not wanting to have this conversation but not able to avoid it now. I pull out one of the stools and sit opposite them so I can see both of their reactions.

"You didn't tell us about her, per se," Pierce says, biting his thumb nail and I know he's hiding something from me.

"Spit it out. Tell me what happened," I say, hoping they rip the bandaid off fast and they are willing to help me deal with whatever went down.

"Okay, I'm going to say it and you can ask questions when I'm done. No interrupting," Pierce says, so I nod, not entirely sure I'm ready to hear it. "You took off from the party after the Avery incident. I looked all over the house for you but no one had seen you. Then I got a call from JP." He winces when he mentions my cousin which can't be good. "He knew you were at Quinn's grave and in a bad way, so I found Xander and we ran all the way to the cemetery. Lucky we got there when we did, because you were about to have a full blown panic attack." I let out a sigh and lower my head, ashamed they saw me like that. "Tate man, we are your best friends. It's nothing to be embarrassed about," Pierce says softly.

"Yeah. We are here for you, anytime you need us," Xander adds.

"Thanks guys," I say, more somber than when I woke up. This night sounds like it ended horribly.

"Come on, get to the best part," Xander chimes in, excitedly.

"There's a best part?" I ask, wearily.

"Yeah, once you calmed down, you were muttering about Sweetness." The mention of her nickname has the hairs on the back of my neck standing up. "Pierce here saw you were on the phone," Xander says, taking the lead on the story.

"Oh shit," I say, realising what must have happened.

"Yeah, you rang her and she's the one who told JP you were at the grave. Pierce talked to her a bit and you admitted she's your green fairy. So there. You have been holding out on us. Why didn't you tell us about her? Oh and you said she was your best friend too," Xander finishes. They both stare at me, with similar wide eyed smiles on their faces. I rub a hand down my face. I can't believe I rang her. I don't remember what I said to her.

"Sooo are you going to tell us about her now?" Xander asks, curiously.

"Nope," I say, hoping they will drop it. I highly doubt it will happen though.

"Come on man, you called her your green fairy. She's the one you want to give your V plates up for. Admit it," Xander pokes, and my throbbing head is getting worse.

"Drop it please. I'll tell you about her another time but not now okay?" I plead, looking between them.

"Admit she's your green fairy first then I'll drop it," Xander says, smirking. My breathing picks up and Pierce must sense it because he fires in on Xander.

"Why don't we talk about how I caught you dry humping Claudia Young against the back of the house?" Pierce says to Xander, and Xander's face turns a crimson red.

"Isn't she the weird girl who claims she's a vampire and drinks blood?" I ask, trying to remember her face to distract myself from thoughts of Tamsyn.

"Yes, that's the one," Pierce says, looking at Xander smugly.

"You weren't supposed to say anything man," Xander sooks to Pierce, and I know Pierce threw Xander under the bus to get him off my back which I'm grateful for. They start playfully arguing about other weird activities she gets up to while Xander defends her. This gives me the perfect chance to make my getaway. I creep back to the couch, lay down and close my eyes. I hope I can fall back to sleep and delay having to contact Tamsyn or JP to find out what happened last night. I'm not ready for that yet.

-- Tamsyn --

I wake up and check the time on my phone. It's nearly lunchtime. I've slept half the day away. I was so wired after hearing Tate's voice, it took forever to fall asleep again. I've missed his voice. I didn't realise how much until I heard it last night. He only rang me because he was drunk but at least I got to hear from him. His pain still sounds extremely raw. My broken boy. I need to think of a way to help him. I meant it when I said I would show him the light out of the darkness. He saved me. It's about time I returned the favour. This time I won't let him push me away.

I snatch my phone up again, a bit more alert now and text JP.

Tamsyn: Have you heard from Tate?

It doesn't take long for him to reply but my heart sinks when he does.

JP: No I haven't. Not sure I will. Do you want me to ring him to see if he's ok?

I don't know what to do. Should I get JP to check on him for me? Or should I let it be? Perhaps he will contact me himself. Surely his friends have filled him in on last nights' events and mentioned me and our phone call. I can only live in hope I guess.

Tamsyn: No that's ok. Let me know if you hear from him.

JP: Will do. You ok?

Tamsyn: Yea fine don't worry about me

JP: I do tho

Tamsyn: I'm fine really

JP: Ok. Here if you want to talk :)

Tamsyn: Thanks

I sit up in bed, replaying last night in my head. He sounded completely lost and broken. I wish he was still close. How can I help him when he's far away? A knock at my door interrupts my thoughts.

"Hey bub, would you like to come to the movies with me? We could grab a late lunch while we are out too. We could make a day of it?" Mum asks.

I've missed hanging out with my mum and we don't get out of the house as much as we used to, so before I can second guess my decision I say, "Sure Mum, sounds great. I'll jump in the shower and get ready."

"Perfect. I'll go get changed," Mum says, before walking towards her room with a huge smile upon her face.

Throwing the covers back, I hop out of bed and walk down the hall to the bathroom. Once I'm under the warm spray, I let the water wash away all my worries over Tate and decide to focus on spending some quality time with my mum instead. I'm sure Tate will contact me if he wants to. I can't dwell on him too much though as it will dig up more hurt, something I don't need at the moment. Turning the water off, I step out and wrap myself in a white fluffy towel, shuffle back to my room and choose an outfit to wear.

Mum and I venture out and dine in for a late lunch at this french bistro, situated close to the movie theatre. Once our bellies can hold no more food, we wander down the road to watch the newest chick flick. It's a nice feeling to be out with Mum again. I don't think we do it enough these days. As she is driving us home, she brings up the subject I least want to talk about. Tate.

"Have you heard from Tate, bub?" she asks, still not knowing he said he wasn't going to return.

Deciding to finally fill her in I say, "Umm Mum, he's not coming back. He said he wasn't going to return once he left." I drop my head in disappointment after hearing it said out loud.

"Aww bub, are you sure he won't change his mind?" she asks, hopeful.

"No Mum, I haven't heard from him properly since he left so I think he's made it clear," I say, failing to keep my emotions in check as they leak out, making me raise my voice.

"Well, I'm sorry to hear that. He was a lovely boy. You know what it's like to lose someone. It's not easy, give him time to find his feet. With

113

the way he looked at you, I'm sure they'll lead him back to you," she says, and I choose not to answer. I could do with a subject change so I distract her by telling her about the skills and life lessons we are going to be participating in over the next few weeks. This occupies the rest of the drive home. I'm thankful she can be easily distracted sometimes.

It's late by the time we arrive home. I'm still full from lunch so I tell Mum I'm going to have an early night then climb the stairs to my room. Flopping onto my bed, I grab the remote and scan through Netflix to find something meaningless which I can drift off to sleep to. I haven't checked my phone since we left the house hours ago. If I'm being honest with myself, I've been too scared to check it. Scared because I know if he didn't text, I'll be disappointed and if he did, I'm worried what it might say. I drag my phone out of my pocket and turn the screen on. My heart skips a beat as there's a text icon flashing. When I open it, disappointment floods through me for a second as it's not the name I wanted to see. It's from Penny.

Penny: Hey wanna hang at mine one day this week?

I can't help but smile. I'm grateful I have Penny. The guys are great and I love hanging out with them but sometimes, a girl needs girl time.

Tamsyn: I'd love that. In desperate need of girl time.

Penny: Yay :)

With our plans sorted, I lie back and click on the first movie I come across. I don't care what it is, I'm using it as a way to keep my mind off other thoughts for a while. In particular, any thoughts of Tate. The movie finished a while ago and I've been lying here not able to sleep. As my eyes get droopy and I'm finding it harder to stay awake, I hear the familiar 'DING DING' of an incoming text. Sleepily I stretch out and grasp my phone from beside my bed. Noticing the name on the screen has me feeling wide awake and alert. Tate's name stares back at me from the glowing screen. My heart is pounding in my chest. I don't know if I'm ready to hear what he has to say. I don't think my heart could handle him pushing me away again. I'm unsure how long I sit, staring at the screen, unable to open his message. Be brave, Tam, I think. I can't ignore it now, can I? I click on the message and hold my breath as I read.

Tate: Hi

Okay, that's not what I was expecting but I can deal with this. Maybe he's as nervous as me.

Tamsyn: Hi

I reply and wait anxiously for what he will say next.

Tate: Can't sleep?

Tamsyn: No. Was taking me a while to fall asleep tonight. You?

Tate: Same

I snuggle down into my bed and pull the covers up, as I tightly hold my phone in the dark. Taking a deep breath in, I decide to follow my advice and be brave. So here goes.

Tamsyn: What's keeping you up?

I stare at the phone, waiting for his reply. It's not instant like the other replies. Is he debating whether to text me? I eagerly open the message when it pops up.

Tate: You

I hold my breath as I continue with my bravado and reply.

Tamsyn: Why am I keeping you up?

Tate: My friends told me I rang you last night but I don't remember any of it. Worried about what I said

Tamsyn: You didn't say anything embarrassing, if that's what you're worried about

Tate: I'm scared to know what I did say

Tamsyn: You were upset about Quinn. It was mainly about her. I just listened.

Tate: The guys said you contacted JP to tell them to find me. Thanks

Tamsyn: It's not a big deal. That's what friends do right?

Tate: Do you still think of us as friends?

Tamsyn: The best of friends

Tate: :) Night Tamsyn

Tamsyn: Sweet dreams, Tate.

Chapter 13

-- Tate --

I lie back on my pillows, staring at the text messages from Tamsyn. Gosh I miss her. I didn't think I would miss her this much. I don't know what I said to her last night because I was too scared to ask her to be specific. I wonder what I said about Quinn. I'm too much of a coward to ask, in case it rips me apart. Did I reveal my inner most thoughts to Tamsyn? Did I confide in her how I'm feeling? These questions will go unanswered because I can't ask her to tell me. I'm too scared of what my drunk self revealed.

Xander picks me up Monday morning for school. As much as I tried to push Tamsyn out of my head, she lingered in my thoughts the rest of the weekend. Xander gives me a knowing smile when I get in the car. Now he knows about Tamsyn, he will never let up until I tell them about her. I'm not sure I'm ready for that.

"Don't mention her because I'm still not ready to tell you guys," I quickly tell Xander, before he can start asking any questions. His face drops because I ruined his plan to bombard me with questions about Tamsyn. Lucky I got in first.

"Fine," he says grumpily, as he pulls away from my house, driving us to school. I want to change the subject so I think of anything I can use to distract him.

"So are you and Claudia a thing now?" I ask smiling, and I see the hint of a smile tug at his lips as he shrugs.

"I don't know man. It was fun hooking up with her but I am not keen for the cooky dooky, wacky dacky, cray cray stuff the chick is into." His reply has me bursting out laughing. The motion feels foreign and I can't remember the last time I full belly laughed like that. Xander openly stares at me. He must be thinking the same thing, as he smiles brightly at me.

"It's nice to see you smile man," he says softly, and I understand the meaning behind his words. If I can't remember the last time I've smiled, I'm sure my friends can't either. We drive the rest of the way with him filling me in on all the other crazy things he's heard Claudia is into. It keeps a genuine smile on my face the whole ride to school.

My happiness is short lived. I didn't think it would last, not with me being in a permanent state of grief but it's the most unlikely thing that rids me of my happiness. Pierce catches up to me in between classes as I'm walking to my maths class. He looks flustered as he rushes towards me.

"Dude, we have a problem," he quickly says, pushing me into the nearest classroom. Thankfully it's empty.

"What's the matter?" I ask, stumbling backwards and managing to catch myself before I fall on my ass. He runs his hand down his face and looks at me with pity, dripping from his eyes.

"Avery is the matter," he replies.

"What has she done now?"

"Umm, it's not so much what she's done. It's what she's insinuating you've done," he says, as his eyes tighten with tension. My stomach drops because when it comes to Avery, I've learnt it usually isn't anything good.

"Spit it out," I tell him, annoyed because Avery is causing stress in my life I don't need. His head drops towards the floor as he mumbles something incoherent. I don't catch anything.

He peeks up at me nervously and I raise my brow at him saying, "I got none of that. Try again."

He lets out a defeated sigh and then slowly tells me, "Avery took pictures of you when you were passed out with her at the party." As his words sink in, I feel the blood leave my face, thinking the worst.

"What pictures?" I desperately ask.

"I haven't seen them but from what I've heard, it looks like you two were getting it on. It's as if she wanted proof this time," he explains, and I try to filter through my thoughts, trying to drum up any memories from that part of the night but it's still blank.

"Damn it. I can't remember anything. You're sure I didn't hook up with her, aren't you?" I ask him, hoping he knows the truth.

"I was outside the room when you came barrelling out of there. You were desperate to get away from her and called her a bloody psycho. She was in her bra though and a few people saw. You know that's all the ammunition people need to start gossiping. They rarely care if it's true, as long as it's juicy," he explains, as I rub the tension out of my neck I feel starting to build up.

"Why can't she leave me alone?" I say, more to myself than Pierce.

He replies with, "Guess she can't get enough of the Tateman." I stare at him unimpressed but then his wide smile takes over his face and I can't help the smile creeping up on mine.

"You're such a dick," I say, shaking my head. "And don't call me that. Man, I can't believe we thought those nicknames were cool," I say, with a chuckle.

"Well, Tateman is way better than P Man. I got the short end of the stick." We look at each other and throw our heads back laughing.

"Where's Xan man?" I say, and it has our laughter continuing.

"Could we have been any dorkier?" Pierce asks, wiping the happy tears from his eyes.

"Verdict is still out on you two I think," I say, smirking and I get rewarded with a light punch to my shoulder.

"Very funny," he says.

"Okay, back to more serious matters. What are we going to do about Avery?" I ask, hoping he has a plan to deal with her.

"I wanted to give you a heads up so you didn't get blindsided by it. Me and Xander are trying to find out how bad the pictures are and then we will go from there," he tells me. I nod in thanks, knowing he would have my back.

"Let's hope we can contain it. This is the last thing I want to deal with right now," I say, giving my neck another squeeze trying to release the tension I can still feel.

"We got you man. I'll see you at lunch." He sticks his closed fist out for me to bump so I oblige and then he leaves to hurry to his class. The ones we are both now late for. I stand alone in the silent class for a minute. My deep breaths are the only sound in the room. My mind starts feeding me the worst possible outcomes those pictures may possess and it's nearly more than I can bear. I grab the handle of the door and with determination, I keep the thoughts at bay, striding to my maths class. I know I'll get in trouble for being late but I have more important things to worry about at the moment.

For the rest of the morning, I ignore the few glances in my direction. It isn't until lunch time I run into Avery. She comes bounding up to me with her slicked back highlighted ponytail, swishing behind her. Her face looks like the cat who got the cream. She's bursting with excitement, thinking she has me cornered in whatever game it is she's playing. What she doesn't know is, I've changed drastically and I think she underestimates me or she doesn't know the person I am anymore. I don't think she ever did. I could care less about her drama and how she's trying to drag me into something I want no part in. It makes me more annoyed than anything else.

As she steps closer she lunges for me, wrapping her arms around my neck and says loudly, "Hey Baby," for the whole cafeteria to hear. I keep my arms pinned to my side, hoping she will get the message and remove herself from me but she doesn't. I unlink her arms from behind my neck and pull them down, placing them by her sides and take a step back. If she wants a scene, she will get a scene.

"I'm not your baby," I say, so everyone can hear. I want this over with so I don't have to deal with her anymore. The room goes quiet and everyone is zoned in on our encounter. She smirks at me thinking she has me where she wants me.

"That's not what you were saying at Jax's party," she coolly says, tilting her head to the side, staring at me. Watching. Waiting. I scan the room searching for Pierce and Xander. I haven't seen them since this morning so they haven't been able to fill me in on what they have found out about the photos. I step in closer to her and lower my voice, so less people can hear.

"Avery, be very careful about what you do next. I've lost my patience when it comes to you," I tell her through gritted teeth.

"When are you going to realise I'm the only girl for you? I won't give you up so easily," she says, smiling at me with the fakest grin on her face. How did I ever think I could like this girl?

"No you aren't, Avery. I don't want you," I tell her straight, hoping she will get the message.

With her smile still firmly in place, she bounces up on her tippy toes and whispers in my ear, "Well little miss blue eyes isn't going to want you now." After delivering her cryptic message, she turns on her heels and walks out of the cafeteria. Little miss blue eyes? What does she mean by that? A few seconds go by and then the whole room is filled with people's phones getting notifications. I can feel the dread wash over me. I don't know how she's done it so fast but she has sent the photos to the whole school. My phone dings a second later. I pull it out of my back pocket and my stomach drops for a second time. I'm staring at the photo Avery must have taken. Avery is in her bra, her skirt is hiked up around her waist, with me underneath her. My eyes are closed, there's a slight smile on my face and my hands are on her waist. I have to admit it doesn't look good at all. I look up from my phone and everyone is staring at me. I feel my laboured breaths beginning so I run out of there before I have a panic attack in front of everyone. That's the last thing I need.

I race out of the doors and nearly bowl over Pierce and Xander who look as shocked as I am.

"Did you get the photo?" I ask them.

"I did," Xander says, wincing.

"My phone is still missing. I lost it at the party, but Xan showed me the photo," Pierce says.

"Damn it," I say, running my hand down my face, wishing I could rewind time and not go to the party. The guys look at me with faces as wrecked as I feel. This is the last thing I want to deal with. "I'm gonna head home for the day," I tell them, wanting to be alone.

"Don't let her win, man," Xander pleads.

"I'm not. I just need to be alone," I tell them. "I'll catch you guys later," I say, turning my back on them and walking down the hall towards the main exit. Lost in my head, it isn't until I'm standing in front of her grave, I realise my feet have led me to Quinn. I sink to my knees and let the tears flow freely and mourn for my other half. The person I desperately need right now. My numb switch has momentarily broken and all the emotions I've kept pushed away, flood through me and it physically hurts my heart. It stabs me, cutting me in half.

"Quinny," I say, crying out for her but knowing it's useless. Thoughts of her green eyes and blonde hair invade my mind. This time I let them be and accept all the thoughts of her, rushing to the surface. In this moment I let myself break and feel the pain of her loss consume me. When I feel my breathing increase, I mentally force myself to control them, focussing on the exhale. I hate being out of control. I need to get a handle on these panic attacks, they can't keep controlling me. I stay on my knees until my breaths calm, then I shift to sit on my butt and draw my knees up, staring at the semi fresh grave. The dirt has lowered but is still rounded. That's how I stay for the rest of the day. Staring at the dirt of my sister's grave, feeling numb again after all the pain has emptied and my tears have run dry. All the pain I'd held in tight has been unloaded and now I'm an empty vessel. I know it won't be long until the pain refills again, seeking for another release. I can only hope no one is there to witness it when I unleash it.

Chapter 14

-- Tamsyn --

The guys pick me up for school on Monday as usual. As we are walking into school, JP grabs me by the elbow, halting my steps. Rafe and Scott turn back to see why we've stopped but JP gives them a head nod and without a word, they keep walking, leaving me alone with JP.

"You alright, JP?" I ask, not knowing why he's stopped me.

"I was going to ask you the same thing," he says, looking down at me with concern. I let out a sigh as I realise what he's referring to.

"I'm fine, really. Tate texted me," I tell him, and I can't help the smile creeping across my face.

His mouth drops open and eyes widen as he says, "What? When?" in disbelief because Tate contacted me. I start walking away knowing he will follow me. I don't want to be late for class.

"He texted me the other night. It was mainly to ask what he said when he was at Quinn's grave," I tell JP, hoping he will drop it.

"Is that all?" he asks, suspiciously.

I feel my cheeks heat up as I say, "I think we are still friends. I'm hoping he will keep texting now."

He lets out a frustrated sigh of his own, saying, "I'm surprised he texted you sober. I don't want you getting your hopes up Tamsyn. We both know he's not in a good headspace. I don't want you getting upset if he disappears again." I slow my steps and face him. Seeing the worry lining his face, I place my fake smile on my face. I had become so accustomed to it in the past, I find it easy to revert back into old patterns.

"I'm honestly okay JP. Don't worry, I'm not expecting much," I lie to him, but I've perfected this facade so he believes it. The only person who saw through my fake smiles isn't here to call me out on it anymore. I hope if he completely disappears again, my heart has recovered enough to take the hit. JP stares at me for a second longer then nods his head, accepting what I've said as truth as we turn to go our separate ways.

It isn't until lunch time I get knocked down, all over again. I hadn't heard from Tate again but that hadn't stopped me from checking my phone constantly for new messages. I grab my tray of food and walk through the door leading outside to the guys bench, where they always have lunch when it's sunny.

As I'm approaching they've got their heads together and are talking in hushed voices. It looks like they are having a secret meeting. I slow my steps in case I intrude on something, not meant for my ears.

They still haven't noticed me and I'm nearly at the table so I blurt out, "Hey guys," to get their attention. It has them all jumping out of their seats with guilty expressions on their faces. What's that about? My eyebrows pinch as I glance at each of them in turn. JP hurriedly shoves his phone into his pocket, piquing my curiosity. "Was there something on your phone you didn't want me to see?" I say with a laugh, trying to play off my interest.

"No, nothing," Rafe says, staring at the bench while Scott looks anywhere but at me. I look to JP, trying to read his blank face. The hairs on my arms stand on end, making a chill run over me and I can feel it in the pit of my stomach. It has something to do with Tate.

"Is it Tate?" I ask, staring JP down. Rafe audibly sighs with his head hung low.

"Don't worry about it Tamsyn," JP tells me, but if it's causing this much angst with them, it must be bad.

"Tell me. What is it? I'm not going to stop until I know what it is. I'll ask Tate myself if I have to," I huff, frustration coursing through me. I slam my tray down on the table, keeping my eyes locked on JP.

"You might as well show her," Scott sadly says.

"No, dont," Rafe yells at JP, trying to stop him.

"She's gonna keep going until she gets her way," Scott retaliates.

"Please JP don't," Rafe begs. Why is he begging JP not to tell me whatever it is? How bad is it? I glance at Rafe and his sad eyes lock on mine. I turn my gaze back to JP and hold out my hand, hoping if I appear confident he will give me his phone. We stay locked in a staring contest for a minute before he relents.

"Fine, but you've been warned. It's not pretty," JP says.

"We don't know what it means," Scott says, and I glance to Rafe as his shoulders hunch over, not saying a word. JP swipes his hand across his phone screen bringing up the thing he doesn't want to show me. He holds it up for me to see and my breath whooshes out of my lungs. My ears block all sound except the thundering of my heart beat. My wide eyes stare at the photo of Tate, his eyes closed but a hint of a smile on his lips. His hair appears longer than it was when he left. I haven't seen him for what seems like forever and he already looks a tad different. It's the girl on top of him in her underwear that has me in shock. Who is she and when was this taken? I don't feel the hand on my shoulder until they shake me.

"Tamsyn you okay? I knew you'd be upset if you saw it. That's why I didn't want you seeing it." I lift my gaze away from the photo and stare into Rafe's concerned eyes instead.

Fake smile in place I say, "Yeah, I'm fine," as I force myself to hand JP back his phone and take a seat at the table.

"I'll get to the bottom of it, Tamsyn. I'm sure it isn't what we're thinking," JP says, trying to comfort me. I take a big bite of my apple so I don't have to answer him. The guys all sit quietly and follow my lead, not talking. We stay like this all through lunch and I retreat further into my shell. I manage to hold in the tears. When the lunch bell rings, I scurry away from them and go straight to my safe place. My sanctuary. I spend the rest of the day, holed up in the stall hugging myself tight, keeping myself together. I don't shed a single tear.

I'm silent all the way home and the guys let me be. They don't try to drag me from where my mind has gone, letting me stay in the bubble for now. I say goodbye to them and walk into my house. I take a deep breath and plaster on my old mask, not wanting to upset my mum. She doesn't need to see how much I'm hurting.

"Hey Mum, my stomach's sore. I'm going to go lie down," I yell to where she is in the kitchen. Her head whips my way, inspecting me.

"You okay bub? Is it a tummy bug?" she queries.

"Yeah, I've felt off all day. I'm gonna try to sleep it off," I tell her, as I step towards the stairs, trying to get away from her quizzical eyes.

"I'll check on you later," she says with a frown, walking back towards the kitchen. I traipse up the stairs, open my door and throw myself at my bed. The door slams shut behind me. I pull my knees into my chest and close my eyes tightly, wishing the memory of that photo wasn't melded in my brain. But it is.

My mum checks on me later before she goes to bed. I tell her I'm feeling better but going to keep sleeping, in the hopes I'll be okay to go to school tomorrow. She turns off my light and shuts my door, leaving me lying in the darkness. Why is it always in the dark where my thoughts take control? The demons wait for the light to diminish so they can invade my mind and make me feel worse. I don't want to lie in here and let my thoughts take over so I creep to the closet and change my clothes. I haven't changed out of my uniform yet. I wiggle my feet into my sneakers. I should start untying the laces before I take them off.

Quietly I open my door and close it behind me, then creep down the stairs. My only thought is to get out of the house which is slowly suffocating me. However, as I walk past the living room, my eye catches the moonbeam shining through the curtain onto the liquor cabinet. It's calling to me. My intentions have changed. I quickly step over to it and grab the already opened vodka bottle. I sneak into the kitchen and I find a plastic bottle in the drawer. Trying to be quiet so I don't alert Mum, I tip the vodka into the plastic bottle and then refill the vodka bottle with water. My mum won't know the difference unless she drinks it. Screwing the cap on my plastic bottle, I return the vodka bottle to the cabinet and make my escape. Sipping the burning liquor down as I race away, my thoughts focus on getting me away from the house. No destination in mind but escape. Scratch that thought, I have the perfect place in mind; my dock.

Once I reach the weathered dock, a cloak of peace rains down on me. Nothing else matters. My footsteps creak as I stride to the edge so I can sit and dangle my feet over, mimicking how me and Dad would sit whenever we ventured to the dock. I take a big gulp to wash away the thought. I wish my dad was here. He'd hate to see me upset over a boy but at least he'd be here to see it. I don't know what advice he would give me. Me and Blake didn't have any problems before my dad died so I was always happy on the boyfriend front. There was never any need to ask him for advice about boys.

Another scorching gulp gets forced down my throat, as my thoughts circle around the one thing I won't let my mind stop on. If I stop, I fear it'll crack me open again and I am only getting back to how I used to be. Happy? Is that what I used to be? I don't know now. My brain is split into time frames. There's me with Blake, Parker, Chloe and Leyla before my dad died. There's me with them after my dad died. There's me, when Tate came along and me, when Tate left. Why am I so affected by people when they leave? Why can't I be me? Tamsyn. No catastrophic changes necessary.

Before I can continue on with my inner ramblings, I hear footsteps behind me. I swing my head around and see someone with their hoodie pulled up over their head, coming towards me. They must see the fear on my face because they quickly pull the hoodie back to show their face. I should have known one of them would find me. I turn back and ignore them as they take a seat next to me.

"How did you find me out here?" I say irritated, because my quiet moment has been invaded. He smirks at me and flicks his nose with his index finger. I roll my eyes at him and gulp down another mouthful. Breathing out between my teeth to rid the burn from my throat. He snatches the bottle from me and takes a sip before I can stop him.

"You shouldn't be drinking out here alone in the dark, Ice Queen," JP says, handing me back the bottle.

"I don't need a lecture. Now, tell me how you found me?" I ask angrily.

He scratches his head and says, "You went quiet on us at school and you didn't return any of my texts. I decided to come to your house to check on you and I saw you running away from it, so I followed you. You should keep an eye on your surroundings. I could have been anyone following you." I roll my eyes at him again as I swallow more vodka down, needing to forget.

"Why do you call me Ice Queen?" I randomly ask. I've always

wondered but he's never confirmed it. His cheeks redden and I can't take my gaze off his pink skin. I don't think I've ever seen JP embarrassed.

"Way to put me on the spot," he says shyly. I raise my brows at him, glad to have the attention off me for a minute. "Remember when I asked you out a few years ago?" he asks, and I nod because I remember it clearly. "You blew me off so badly in front of everyone. I didn't take it very well and wanted to hurt you so I came up with the silly nickname for you. You were quite mean back then," he says, laughing as he grabs my bottle for another sip, probably needing the alcohol to numb himself after his confession.

"I'm sorry. I was only mean about it because Chloe liked you at the time and I didn't want to hurt her feelings by going out with you," I confess, holding out my hand to get the bottle back from him.

His nose wrinkles in disgust as he says, "Chloe? No. I'd never have gone out with her. She was way more of a bitch than you were." His reply has us both cackling with laughter. Once we stop laughing, he clarifies with a cheeky grin, "You aren't a bitch anymore."

"Thanks. I probably still have her hiding somewhere deep inside of me," I tease. He offers me a small smile.

"Nah, I think the Ice Queen thawed a while ago," he says, staring at me. We both break our gaze at the same time, turning our view out to the calm water. It looks as if it stretches out for miles into the darkness. "You okay?" he asks quietly, and I hear the question without him saying it out loud. He's asking about the photo. I came out here to forget, not to have it dragged to the surface. The hurt I'd managed to push down bubbles up and my eyes burn. I turn to him with blurred vision and his face drops as he puts his arm around my shoulder, encasing me in his arms. Having him comfort me, forces the tears to leak out and drip down onto my shirt. He softly places his fist under my chin and lifts my gaze up to his. His thumb glides across my cheeks, one at a time, wiping the tears away.

"It hurts," I confess, and the tears force themselves down my face in a flurry. Luckily JP is there to cuddle me.

"It'll be okay, I promise," he says, rubbing my back up and down, calming my sobs which are slowly turning into sniffles.

"Have you heard from him?" I ask, dreading his answer but it's worse not knowing.

"No, his phone is switched off, which is weird. It wasn't him who sent me the photo either. It was his friend Pierce." My breath catches at the name Pierce. His friend from the other night. JP must mistake my intake of breath for something else because then he says, "The whole thing feels off to me. Pierce isn't messaging back or answering my calls. I know it's hard but try not to jump to any conclusions until we get the full story from Tate, okay?" I nod, knowing my mind will jump to the worst possible conclusions. I have no control over it in this situation.

"I miss him," I sadly say.

"I know. I miss him too," JP says, squeezing me closer to him. I can feel my brain getting hazy, the longer we sit here. The vodka finally kicking in.

"So do you like Penny?" I blurt. The vodka is loosening my lips if nothing else. He throws his head back laughing.

"Why, has she said something about me?" he asks, not giving anything away.

"Maybe. Maybe not," I drag out, and he laughs again.

"Would it be an issue, if I did like her? Our friendship is the most important thing right now Ice Queen. So if it bothers you, I won't go there. I won't even entertain the thought," he says, and his words have me staring at his face.

"When did our friendship become the most important thing to you? You hated me not too long ago," I say, not believing what he's saying. He links our hands together, giving mine a squeeze. He gazes upwards while he talks.

"For the longest time I thought you were horrible. Then Tate came along and was always telling me there was more to you. I kept pushing him when it came to you because I didn't want you to hurt him, how you'd hurt me. The day I went off at you in the car park and then seeing you so broken in the shower afterwards," he draws a big breath in and drops his head as he continues, "It was the worst day of my life. I felt responsible for breaking you." He tilts his head to me and admits, "I still feel responsible."

"I told you it was a lot of things that caused me to snap," I say, trying to soothe him.

"Yeah but I was one of those factors. So since then, I've felt protective of you. I never want you to feel that low again Tamsyn. I see how Penny makes you happy and I don't want to jeopardize your friendship with her."

"It won't," I tell him.

"How can I be sure though? You're quite good at covering up how you are feeling," he says, and I realise he saw through my fake smile today. He chose not to say anything in the moment about it. Maybe the observation skills run in his family.

"I promise if I ever feel that low again, I'll reach out to someone, okay?" I say, holding out my pinky finger for him.

He stares at it, his lips tugging up at the corners as he brings his own pinky to mine, linking them and saying, "Pinky promise."

"Now back to Penny, do you like her?" I ask, eagerly.

"What did I just say? I don't want me going out with her to affect your friendship if something happens," he says.

"If you treat her right, we won't have a problem," I say, winking at him or it could be squinting. The alcohol is running full force through me now. "I give you my blessing," I say matter of factly, causing him to laugh loudly.

"Come on, think it's time you went to bed," he says, as he jumps to his feet and then pulls me up to stand next to him. I sway a bit so he puts his arm around my shoulder to steady me. We walk like that, throwing my now empty bottle in the bin as we go.

"Tamsyn, I meant what I said about Tate. I know him. There must be more to the story," he says, as we arrive at my house.

"Okay, I'll try not to let my thoughts run wild," I say to him.

"You going to be alright getting inside?" he asks, and I nod.

"Probably be quieter, me going in alone. Although, Rafe has managed to get me to bed twice now, without being seen," I say.

"That's because Rafe is used to sneaking in and out of girls' houses," he whispers right outside my door, and I have to cover my mouth with my hand to hold in my laughter.

"True. Goodnight JP. Thanks for following me. I feel better now," I tell him.

He steps away from me and as I turn the door handle to go inside, he whispers, "Night, Ice Queen." I close the door behind me as he walks away from my house. I tiptoe upstairs, shrug out of my clothes then climb into bed. My brain swirls around, making me dizzy as the alcohol flows through my system. The alcohol does its job, drowning out any worries I had of Tate, and letting me drift off into a forgetful slumber.

Chapter 15
~

-- Tate --

I can't face school on Tuesday so I spend it in bed. Mum comes into my room in the morning since I never got up. I tell her I need a day off and she doesn't push for any more information. I'm grateful. I've had my phone turned off since I left school yesterday. I didn't want anyone texting me about the stupid photo. It makes me furious thinking about the lengths Avery has gone to. Why can't she accept the fact I don't want to be with her?

My mind is all over the place and without thinking it through, I slide Quinn's journal out from under my pillow. It's been hiding there for weeks now. I haven't opened it again since I took it from her room, scared of what other secrets I may find. At this point in time, I need a connection to my sister. Her own written words are the closest I can get right now.

I sit up, fluff my pillows behind me and lean back. Holding her precious journal in my hands, I take a deep breath and center myself before I flip open the cover. I scan pages as I flick through. A lot of what is written are random quotes; quotes about life and happiness. As I flip through, I notice the context of the quotes change. They change from happiness to depression, sadness and hope. My breathing picks up pace but I breathe deeper, staying in control. My flicking stops on a random page in the middle of the book. It doesn't look any different to the other pages except the title catches my eye. It says Dear Quinn. I hold my breath, close my eyes and lean my head back against the wall. I don't know if I have the strength today to open up something not meant for my eyes. Before my heart can tell my mind to stop, my eyes begin reading what it says.

Dear Quinn,

You are stronger than you possibly know. You need to pull yourself out of this darkness you are living in and see you are loved and worthy of love. You are a beautiful soul who deserves all life has to offer so stop the darkness from taking hold. Fight it with all you have inside. You can do it. I believe in you. Remember that when you feel yourself start to fade.

You have your friends, your family and everyone who loves you. You have Tate. Reach out to them when you need to. Don't hold it in. Don't feel guilty for the way you feel either. Try to be kinder to yourself because you are too hard on yourself. Love who you are and everything about yourself because the people in your life, love you just as you are. Don't lose hope. Hang on and find the light again.

I hope you are fighting the darkness.

Love, Quinny xx

She wrote this to herself? My stiff grip on the journal loosens and it drops to my lap. I swipe at the wetness covering my cheeks. My poor Quinny. Why did I not see how much she was hurting inside? I wish I had listened to her more. I drop my head into my hands and let my tears fall freely. Her words cut me. The words hit a nerve, it's like she was talking directly to my soul. Why do I connect with what she's written in this book?

I've been feeding the darkness inside me, using it to keep myself numb. It's twice now Quinn has mentioned darkness and her version isn't something I want to deal with. Why did she have to lose her struggle with it? I would have fought it for her, if I could have. Does she know that, wherever she is? Does she know I would have done anything to save her? Tremors shake my body as the pain is unleashed. Everything I've contained is released. It's as if yesterday spent crying at her grave wasn't enough of a release. How much pain is held inside of me? When will I have let enough out to stop the tears?

Her words echo in my head. Stop the darkness taking hold, persevere, don't give in. It's time I take her advice. My sister's words can't be in vain, can they? Did she put them there to save me? Does she want me to learn from her mistakes? Can I manage to pull myself out of the darkness? Sparkling blue eyes trickle through my mind and I hold the image in my head. Is she the light I need to hold on to? Is Tamsyn the key to unlock my cage?

Gathering the book up, I gently slide it back under my pillows and lie down, curled on my side. I think that's more than enough insight into Quinn's mind today. Thinking of Quinn brings a fresh wave of tears and I let it out, taking my twin's advice. I see now how easy it is to hold the darkness in and keep it to yourself but I'm only feeding it this way. Isn't there a famous quote by Martin Luther King Jr where he says, 'Darkness cannot drive out darkness; Only light can do that.' He's right. I need the light to help me through this dark storm of grief I'm going through.

I lie there wrapped in my thoughts. I pushed Tamsyn away, thinking she was hurting me by making me feel too much but is it possible that's what I needed? I needed to let the hurt and pain out and she forced it out of me, when I thought I knew better. Was she the light all along? I couldn't see it through my grief because I wasn't thinking clearly.

I sit up, with my epiphany swimming in my head. I miss Tamsyn so much. Should I reach out to her? She lost her dad so she knows what it's like to lose someone. I think I'll give it another day before I text her. I've had enough of an emotional outlet for today. I snuggle back into my bed and push my thoughts down, closing my eyes to get some sleep. All the crying has left me exhausted.

I wake later and my room is darker than it was earlier. I throw back the covers and swing out of bed, feeling a fraction lighter than I did this morning. As I stagger to the kitchen I spot my mum bent over the stove, inspecting something in a pot. She must hear me because she whips around with a small smile, lifting the corner of her mouth.

"Are you hungry honey? Dinner's almost ready," she says, and I glance out the window to see the sun is indeed setting and nightfall is closing in.

"I didn't realise I slept so long," I say to Mum. She turns to me, her smile laced with tension.

"You probably needed it." Does she know I haven't been sleeping well since Quinn died? Is it the same for her?

A voice in my head sings, 'Reach out,' and I force myself to say, "I haven't slept great since Quinn died," while looking at the table. I hear Mum's soft steps towards me and then she's wrapping her arms around my shoulders. I return her hug and squeeze her tight.

We stay wrapped in each other's embrace for a while before she says, "Me too, honey. Me too." I hold her a bit tighter, knowing we both need each other more than ever. I haven't talked to my parents about Quinn and they don't force me to talk to them. Maybe that's the problem, we need to talk about her. Holding each other for a while, the sound of our breaths is the only thing we can hear. I slowly loosen my grip on Mum and she does the same, walking back over to her pot.

I stand up, follow her steps and ask, "Do you need a hand? What's for dinner?" My questions are rewarded with a bright smile.

"You can cut the tomatoes up if you like?" she says, and I nod. I grab some tomatoes, place them on the board and start cutting.

Turning my head over my shoulder I softly say, "I love you, Mum."

Her eyes glisten at me with unshed tears as she says, "I love you too." With a small smile on my face, I go back to cutting my tomatoes, feeling a lightness in my soul.

Don't Panic. Keep Breathing.

Chapter 16

~

-- Tamsyn --

A throbbing head greets me on Tuesday morning. I peel my eyes open to locate my phone. My wretched alarm is poking holes in my brain. I dismiss it and quickly check but there are no new texts. I throw my head back against my pillow, wishing I knew what those photos meant. No matter how much I tell myself not to worry about them, I can't help it. My brain has a mind of its own and it's running wild. I need to distract myself from thoughts of Tate so I text Penny. Girl time is what I need.

Tamsyn: Hey chicky, hang out after school? Need girl time x

I leave my phone on my bedside table and drag myself to the bathroom. I swallow down a couple of paracetamol for my headache and jump in the shower. I close my eyes and let the warm water wake me up. I need all the help I can get today. Wrapping myself in a towel, I check my phone once back in my room and Penny has replied.

Penny: Yay. Can't wait :)

With a huge smile on my face, I have a new vigour to carry me through the day. I get dressed quickly and have enough time to grab a slice of toast on my way out the door to meet the guys. I don't think my stomach could handle coffee right now so I go without.

As I slide into my seat in the back, JP gives me a knowing smile through the rear view mirror.

"How are you feeling today Tamsyn?" he says, failing to hold his smirk back.

I roll my eyes at him as I reply, "Just peachy," and can't help but return his smile. Rafe looks between us, raising his brows.

"Did I miss something?" he asks, his head snapping back and forth.

"Nah, nothing bro" JP tells him. He mustn't have mentioned last night to Rafe which has me smiling inside. It's nice to know I can rely on these guys to keep my secrets from everyone, even each other.

"I don't need a ride home after school. I'm hanging out with Penny," I inform them, so they don't wait for me.

"Ugh, I hate missing out when you guys have girl time," Rafe says, pouting as he raises his fingers to make imaginary speech marks when he says girl time, like it's a bad thing.

"If you like I can paint your nails and braid your hair some time Rafe," I say, giggling behind my hand.

"You'll have to find a colour to suit my complexion," Rafe says, playing along. "It may have to be tiny braids too. My hair isn't as long as yours," he says, winking at me. With a full heart, I push the thoughts of Tate away and surprisingly manage to enjoy my day.

As me and Penny sit on her couch gossiping about other people at school, I build up the courage to ask her opinion about Tate. She wasn't at lunch with us yesterday as she was in the library working on an assignment. I'm not sure if the guys shared the photo with her either.

"Hey Pen, the guys didn't mention the photo of Tate to you, did they?"

"No, what photo?" she asks, looking up from painting her toenails an aqua colour. I cringe as the image pops into my head but I've already broached the subject. I better continue otherwise she will hound me until I give in now.

"Umm it was of Tate and there was a half naked girl on top of him," I cringe, because it sounds worse coming out of my mouth. Penny's angry gaze snaps to me.

"What?" she roars, screwing the lid back on the nail polish and putting it on the coffee table. Her feet stamp the carpet as she sits up straighter giving me her full attention. "Who had it?"

"I caught JP showing Rafe and Scott at lunch yesterday," I tell her, wringing my hands in my lap. "They tried to hide it from me. They didn't want me getting upset."

"Tell me exactly what was in the picture," she demands, so I explain exactly what I saw. I tell her how the photo showed Tate with some beautiful girl in her bra, straddling him and him smiling. She moves to my side and puts her arm over my shoulder.

"Have you asked Tate about it?" she asks, quietly.

"JP said he'd tried contacting him yesterday but Tate's phone was off. I was too much of a coward to try myself," I confess.

"How'd they get the photo in the first place?"

"One of Tate's best friends sent it to JP," I tell her, and she leans back, her brows creasing in the middle of her forehead.

"Well, that's weird," she says.

"What do you mean?"

"It's weird. Tate is crazy about you. Anyone with half a brain could see he was. His best friend must know that. So why on Earth would he send the photo to JP, knowing you might potentially see it? It would hurt you and hurt Tate. It doesn't make sense. Unless he's not a very good friend?" she rambles, without taking a breath.

"The best friend sounded nice when I spoke to him," I tell her.

"When did you speak to his best friend?" she asks me, and I visibly cringe again because I haven't told her about the other night. I didn't think it was right to break Tate's trust and tell anyone about him being at Quinn's grave.

"Umm the other night. Tate rang me while drunk. Long story short, his friend came on the phone and he sounded like a good friend," I tell her, biting my nails.

"What are you not telling me?" she quizzes.

"That's Tate's business. Tate needed help and the friend was good about it. I don't think he would send the photo knowing it would hurt Tate," I tell her.

She claps her hands, "There you have it then. If you don't think the best friend did it to hurt Tate, then there has to be more to the story. I'd say wait until you hear from Tate before you start cutting him out of your life," she says, winking at me. She's right. The photo came from Pierce and I don't believe he'd do anything to hurt Tate, not after I heard the way he was with Tate. Especially when he was having his panic attack. There's gotta be more to it. But it still doesn't explain the photo. Something clearly happened. Girls don't magically appear on top of guys. I push my worries aside and try to enjoy the rest of my time with Penny.

-- Tate --

Lying in bed Tuesday night, I decide to be brave and face whatever is waiting for me on my phone. Turning it on, I'm bombarded by an extreme amount of notifications. I wait until they stop to see if there's anything important. I scan through the messages and instantly delete ones from Avery without looking at them. Nothing from Tamsyn is in my inbox. There's a few missed calls from JP, Rafe and Scott so I open JP's messages to see what he was calling about. As I read his messages, my heart skips a beat and cotton wool blocks my ears.

JP: Bro you need to stop talking to her half arsed and man up

He sent this one Monday morning. I must not have seen it before I switched my phone off. Pierce said it was JP who called him and told him where I was. Obviously it was Tamsyn who told JP, so of course he knew I'd talked to her. Did she mention the fact I'd texted her as well?

JP: What the hell man? What's this photo about?

My heart sinks as I realise they have seen the photo.

JP: Why's your phone off? Get back to me when you get this. Tamsyn has seen it

JP: Are you hiding because you're guilty?

JP: I really hope you aren't hooking up with random chicks to make yourself feel better.

JP: You can't just be there when it suits you. Friends are there all the time and you two were more than friends. If you can't be real with her then leave her alone

JP: Either drop it and let her go on with her life or come back. What you are doing is tearing her to pieces

I quickly read through Scott and Rafe's messages too and they are more or less the same. They've all seen the photo and they can see how affected Tamsyn is by it. They are all forcing me to either choose her or let her go completely.

My heart throbs at the thought of letting her go. How I ever thought I could live without her is beyond me. I wanted to take another day before I contacted her but I don't have time on my hands now. I hate to think what thoughts have been running through her head after seeing the photo. The big question is how the hell did they get the photo in the first place?

I dial JP and wait.

"Where the hell have you been? I've been texting and calling you since yesterday bro," he yells into the phone.

"Sorry man, I turned my phone off. Needed a breather," I say, already dreading this conversation.

"What's up with the photo man? Who's the girl?" My head drops to my chest knowing it's the same photo I've been avoiding since yesterday.

"How did you get it?" I ask.

"Pierce sent it to me. So explain it bro because Tamsyn isn't saying much but I know she's hurting."

"Pierce sent it?" I ask, confused.

"Yeah, he sent it yesterday at lunch time," he says as my mind filters back. I remember running from the cafeteria when Pierce said he hadn't seen the photo because he lost his phone.

"Nah it wasn't Pierce. He lost his phone so someone used his phone to send it to you," I say, not understanding why someone would do that.

"Why would someone send me the photo? The only person who

would get hurt by seeing the photo is Tamsyn," he says, and my brain clicks into place.

"Did you ever text Pierce about Tamsyn?" I hurriedly ask, and I hear JP sigh.

"Yeah I did. The night after you went to Quinn's grave. I texted him to say Tamsyn was worried about you so I asked if you were okay. He replied asking if she was the girl you were seeing while you were here and I said yes," he explains.

"Anything else?" I ask.

"He asked what she looked like so I sent a photo of Tamsyn to him. Why? What's going on?"

"Damn it. It was Avery. She must have Pierce's phone. She mentioned something about little miss blue eyes which I didn't understand at the time. It makes sense now. She was talking about Tamsyn," I tell him.

"Who's Avery?" he asks.

"She's the girl in the photo. She was a friend of Quinn's and we were hooking up for a brief time but I called it off when she got too full on. Now she thinks she can get me back."

"Is the photo true though? Did you hook up with her?" he asks.

"No. From what Pierce said I was drunk out of my mind and she dragged me into a room. Then Pierce said I came storming out of the room, telling him to keep her away from me," I try to explain.

"You don't remember?" he asks.

"No. I was out of my mind drunk, man. It happened the same night I ended up at Quinn's grave and rang Tamsyn. I don't remember my conversation with her or how I got to the cemetery," I sadly tell him, and he stays silent for a minute.

"Are you sure there isn't any truth to the photo?" I let out a breath and close my eyes.

"I don't know man. I feel like I would know if I'd gotten with her. She's hell bent on messing things up for me right now," I say, angrily.

"What are you going to say to Tamsyn?" he asks, letting out a sigh. I know he's worried about me hurting her more.

I want to get to the bottom of this now so I say, "I'm gonna go get the truth from Avery okay? I'll call you later," I say in a hurry.

"Okay bro, talk soon," he says, and the line goes dead.

I don't want to wait for answers, not now I know this whole situation is hurting Tamsyn too. My only thought now is fixing things with her. I never wanted to cause her pain and I won't let Avery of all people tear my Sweetness down. I slip on my shoes, chuck on a sweatshirt and yell out to Mum and Dad to let them know I'm going out for a run. When my feet hit the pavement, they take me a few blocks over to Avery's house.

I knock harshly on the familiar door then step back and wait. Avery's little sister Annie answers the door, greeting me with a huge smile.

"Tate," she squeals, throwing herself at me. She was always hanging around Avery and Quinn and would get dragged over to our house a lot.

"Hey Annie, is Avery home?" I ask, setting her back on her feet after I give her a small squeeze.

She turns over her shoulder and yells, "Avery, Tate's here." I hear the quick footsteps of Avery racing to the door. A giant smile ignites on her face once she sees me.

"Tate! It's so good to see you," she says, as she tries to hug me but I step back and her smile drops.

148

"Annie, can you give us a minute please? Avery, can I talk to you outside please?"

Both sisters say, "Sure." Avery steps out of the door and Annie steps back in, closing the door behind her.

"So have you come to your senses?" Avery asks, in what she thinks is a seductive voice.

"Cut the crap Avery. I know you've got Pierce's phone and sent my cousin the photo. Hand the phone over." Her eyes bulge and I see the vein in her temple sprout to the surface. The vein clued us in when we were younger that she was about to go nuclear. She crosses her arms over her chest.

"I don't know what you're talking about?" she grits out, knowing she's been called out on her lies. I can't take it anymore. Staring at this girl, who Quinn called a best friend, makes me furious with how she is acting now and I snap.

"Avery, my sister fucken died," I scream at her, and she takes a step back. Startled, she drops her arms to her side, waiting to see what I'll do next. "She died and you were supposed to be her best friend. What kind of friend, especially a best friend, does this shit? Tell me because I'm clueless," I yell, my body heaving with the pent up emotions I'm throwing at her.

"I uh I umm..." she mumbles. I close my eyes and rub my forehead trying to ease the headache she is causing.

"Did you ever care about me or was I just a game to you?" I demand.

"Of course I care about you," she says, quietly.

"Well you have a funny way of showing it. If you gave a damn about me or Quinn, you wouldn't be doing this. I'm fucken messed up over Quinn. I don't need this bullshit in my life. You need to let it go. We are never going to be together. Just let me grieve for my sister in peace," I yell, and then wait, staring at the girl in front of me who I feel nothing for.

She starts sniffling and says, "I'm sorry. I like you and I thought we were good together," she tries to reason.

"Avery please. For my sake, let it go. Give me Pierce's phone and we can put all this behind us," I plead, my vision becoming blurry from unwelcome tears I didn't want her to see.

The tears must win her over because she lets out a sigh and says, "Fine. It was me who sent the photo to your cousin off Pierce's phone. Wait here, I'll grab it." She rushes inside and is back a minute later. She holds it out for me and I take it.

"So you set the whole thing up with the photo?" I quiz her. It's the reason I came over after all; to learn the truth.

She chuckles before saying, "It was easy. You were so wasted. I thought it would take a lot more to get you alone. I snapped the photos then you started going on about blue eyes and pushed me off and ran out of the room," she says, still frustrated about the whole thing.

"So we didn't hook up?" I need it clarified. She shakes her head.

"No we didn't. Will that help you sleep at night?" Jeez this girl is a whole other level of psycho.

"Yes it will," I say, relief washing over me.

I turn to leave and she says, "I don't know what you see in her. She's not pretty at all," she snarls at me. I smile back as I leave because she doesn't need to see what I see. No one does. It's what drew me to Tamsyn in the first place. I saw something in her no one else did. She will always be beautiful in my eyes. How can she not be when she's my light in the darkness. She's the one my soul craves. I can try to deny it all I want but it's still there. I wish it hadn't taken me this long to come to my senses.

I spend the rest of the evening racing around, sorting things out. My first stop is Pierce's where I hand him back his phone and fill him in on what Avery did. He checks his phone and sure enough, the evidence is there. She didn't think to delete the texts she sent JP. They were still there for anyone to see.

Next, I ring JP on my way home from Pierce's and explain everything to him. After I told him Avery confirmed we didn't hook up, he reiterated what he said in his texts. I have to make a decision. If I was in Tamsyn's life, then I was in. I couldn't disappear or push her away again. If I couldn't be the person she needed me to be then he wanted me to give her up. It was not an option I wanted to consider. Not after I'd realised how much I need her. I need her like she needed me. She never asked for my help. I gave it willingly but now I need hers. After pushing her away, I don't care if I have to resort to begging. I will do whatever it takes.

-- Tate --

Ilay in bed that night wondering what I should say to her. How do I explain the photo to her? I'm still a mess but JP's words echo in my thoughts. How can I be what she needs when I can't deal with this grief? I won't let it in most days. Maybe that's my problem. By shutting the grief out, I am making it worse. How can I willingly unleash the pain on my heart when I know it will break me? Am I able to endure the anguish so I can be who Tamsyn needs me to be? I can try. I can do it for her and for me. Will her light be enough to pull me through?

I keep second guessing myself and the clock keeps ticking. It's eleven o'clock now and I still haven't found the courage or sorted out what I'm going to say to her. With sweaty hands I send her a short text message to see if she is still awake.

Tate: Hi

I don't have to wait long before her reply pops up.

Tamsyn: Hi

I smile to myself in the dark and sink deeper into the blankets. Falling back into our familiar pattern is easy. I can do this.

Tate: Can't sleep?

Tamsyn: No. You the same?

I get the urge to hear her voice and before I can stop myself, I'm calling her number and holding the phone to my ear, eagerly waiting for her to answer.

"Hi," she shyly says, and I swear my heart sighs out loud. A feeling of ease takes over me which only she can ignite.

"How are you?" I ask, suddenly at a loss of how to bring up the conversation.

"I'm okay," she replies, her fall back answer. She'd say that even when her world was falling apart.

"The photo wasn't what you think," I blurt out, and bite down on my fist to stop myself from blurting out anything else. I hear her sharp intake of breath.

She's silent for a beat before she says, "Tate, it's fine if you are seeing someone, you don't need to explain." I can hear the sadness behind her words. I wish she wasn't hurting right now because of me.

"I'm not, I wouldn't," I ramble, my brain not able to keep up with my mouth. She stays silent while I gather my thoughts. "Can I explain please?" I beg.

"Okay," she softly says.

"So there's this girl Avery, she was Quinn's best friend. I was hooking up with her before Quinn did what she did." I still can't bring myself to say she committed suicide because that's what she did. She lay in a hospital bed for weeks after the fact but it is still what ultimately led to her death. It is a hard pill to swallow, it probably always will be. I take a big breath and continue. "I called it off when I realised I shouldn't be messing around with Quinn's friend. Plus she got a bit too full on." I stop for a beat to give her time to process my words before I carry on. "When I came back here, she thought I'd want to get back with her but that's not the case. I don't want her." I want you, I say in my head. Can she hear my unspoken words? "She couldn't take me rejecting her. I went to a party and got so drunk, she dragged me into a room and set those pictures up. She admitted it to me tonight. She also clarified that we didn't do anything. She found Pierce's phone at the party and she's the one who sent JP the photo. She sent it to everyone at my school," I say, still frustrated at what lengths she went to.

"Why did she send the photo to JP?" she asks, quietly.

"Because she found out about you and wanted to hurt you. I'm sorry Tamsyn, it's all my fault," I mumble, not sure what else to say.

"When was the photo taken?" she asks.

"It was the other night when I rang you from Quinn's grave," I whisper my confession. I still have a hard time mentioning her name. My heart thunders in my chest. We sit there listening to the other person breathing, both lost in our own thoughts.

She breaks the silence saying, "Okay, I believe you," and my thundering heart nearly leaps out of my chest.

"I'm sorry," I say again.

"It's fine," she says, trying to ease my guilt.

"No it's not. I'm truly sorry it hurt you. You should have never had to see the photo. I don't want you to think the worst of me," I plead, hoping she hears how sorry I am in my voice.

She lets out an audible breath and says, "Tate, you don't have to explain yourself to me. You can do what you want." The hurt I have caused her is still evident in her strained voice. I feel like I'm losing her and I don't know what to say to get her back. I need her more than ever.

If she doesn't believe me now, I need to show her how much I need her. In the cloak of darkness, I siphon all the courage I have inside and whisper her words to me. The same ones she never remembered from our first conversation. I need her to help save me because I can't save myself. I need her to save me before I'm completely lost to the darkness.

"Would you save me if I was drowning?" I ask. Time stands still, her rushed breaths are the only sound. I focus on her inhale and exhale, waiting for her reply. My own breaths speed up but I force myself to gain control. How can I move forward if I can't control this part of me?

"Yes," is her soft reply, and my heart sighs.

"Promise?" I ask. Knowing her memory holds no recognition of our former conversation when the tables were turned.

"I promise," she meekly says. Emotions bubble up in me and my hand shakes, holding the phone. I wriggle down further in the bed, trying to hide in case anyone else can hear my secrets I dare to speak out loud.

"Sweetness?" I shudder.

"Yeah?"

"I'm drowning," I sob, and the floodgates burst open, releasing all the hurt and pain out of me. Opening up and letting someone in is a release in itself.

"I'm here Tate. I'm here," I hear Tamsyn say on the line, trying to comfort me. I hear her own sniffles between my cries and that's how we stay for I don't know how long. Two broken souls connected through a phone line. One trying to comfort the other from miles away. "Let it all out Tate, you can't hold it in," she whispers, and the more I cry, the more overwhelmed I become. A switch flips and my breaths turn short and sharp. No, not now. I have control over this, don't I? I try to control my breathing but it doesn't work. With my heart beating faster, I try drawing breaths into my lungs but it's futile, it feels suffocating.

"Tate!" I hear her firmly scream. "Don't think, remember. Turn it off now. That's enough," she tells me. Don't think. I'd forgotten my mantra but she remembers and says the words I need to hear. Don't think. Don't think. Don't think. I repeat, pushing all my thoughts to the side and focussing on her instead. "Just breathe, Tate. Keep breathing. That's it," she repeats, until I get my breathing under control. "I've got you Tate. I'm here," she says softer, patiently letting me calm myself down in my own time. "I'm here," her wobbly voice whispers.

I don't want to talk anymore, feeling drained from my outlet. I wish she was here in my arms.

"Can we stay on the line until we fall asleep?" I shyly ask, my confidence lacking now when it comes to this girl who has become my anchor; in a sea full of pain. She's keeping me from drifting out into the wide ocean of darkness.

"I'm not going anywhere Tate, sleep now. I'll be here," she gently says, and I close my eyes while keeping my phone to my ear. Listening to her soothing breaths, calms me and lulls me into a welcome sleep.

Don't Panic. Keep Breathing.

Chapter 18

-- Tamsyn --

Sleepily I rub my eyes before peeling them open, still in a daze. I stretch my arms and legs out, releasing the tightness in my stiff body. Turning my head it hits a cold, hard surface. Flipping my body over, I see my phone lying on my pillow and the memory of last night washes over me.

Clumsily grabbing it, I see the call is still going so I put it to my ear and say, "Tate?"

"Hi," is all he says, sounding wide awake. A warmth spreads through my body as a smile widens on my face.

"You're still there?" I say, amazed neither of our phones accidentally hung up during the night.

"Yeah, I'm still here," he says quietly.

"How long have you been awake?" I ask, because he sounds more awake than I feel.

"Long enough to hear your cute little snores," he says, chuckling.

"Hey, I don't snore," I protest, and he laughs so loud, my breath catches. It's been forever since I've heard him laugh.

"Don't worry, I won't tell anyone. It'll be our little secret," he says, with a smile in his voice which keeps my own smile firmly in place.

"Such a comedian today, aren't you?" I add with sarcasm, and I hear his chuckle. "It's good to hear you laugh," I blurt, and I hear his exhale.

"It feels good to laugh too," he sadly replies. "Thanks Tamsyn."

"Anytime. That's what best friends are for," I say.

"Well best friend, I would love to keep chatting but I better get ready for school or I'll be late," he says, with a hint of sadness. I quickly glance at the time on my phone and realise he's right. I'll be late too if I don't get a move on.

"Yeah I better go too," I say, reluctant to hang up.

"Have a good day Tamsyn," he says, and my heart throbs a bit because he's gone back to calling me Sweetness occasionally instead of all the time. It's a start though.

"You too, Tate," I say, as I hang up. I rush to get ready and make it downstairs to meet the guys in the car at record speed. I've never gotten ready for school so fast before.

When I slide into my seat in the car, I must look like a whirlwind. I didn't have enough time to tie up my hair.

"Wow, what's got you all flustered this morning?" Rafe points out.

"Woke up late. I don't look too bad, do I?" I ask, which has Rafe turning to face me from the front as JP pulls the car away from the curb.

He stares at my face for a minute before saying, "Nope, as beautiful as ever Petal," and winking at me. My wide smile shines at him and I catch JP watching me, with a smile of his own in the rear view mirror.

"From your smile, I take it you sorted things with Tate?" JP asks, and I nod.

"Yeah he explained the photo," I tell them, not saying anything else about our conversation.

"Avery sounds like a right little witch, doesn't she?" Rafe says, and I can't help but crack up.

"Yes she does," I say, and sit back in my seat, relaxing. I hope Tate and I have turned a corner. I couldn't handle it if he pushed me away again.

It's Wednesday morning so Rafe, JP and I walk to our first aid lesson which I'm excited for. The class was more fun than I thought it would be. Lily and Zac greet us as we enter and we take our seats as we wait for the last few people to arrive.

"Welcome back everyone. Today we are going to be learning an important part of first aid, CPR. Can anyone tell me what CPR stands for?" Lily asks, directing her question to the group. Everyone gives her a blank stare so she continues. "CPR stands for cardiopulmonary resuscitation. It's an emergency procedure where we use mouth to mouth respirations combined with chest compressions. This helps deliver oxygenated blood to vital organs such as the heart and brain. Zac here is going to demonstrate on our lovely CPR dummy while I talk you through it." Zac drags the dummy in front of our semi circle and positions himself on his knees.

"CPR is important because if you can give someone CPR correctly for a few minutes before help like us arrives, you can save their life. What we are teaching you is a tool to help buy the victim time for help to arrive." Everyone is listening intently to what Lily has to say.

"Before you dive straight into CPR, you need to assess the situation and make sure you are safe yourself before you proceed. For example if there are fallen power lines around, you shouldn't attempt anything. You would need to wait for emergency services. It's up to you to make the call on whether the situation is safe for you to proceed. If you deem it safe, you can either remove the hazard or remove the victim from the danger. Is everyone still with me?" she asks and we all nod.

"Okay, so you've called emergency services and you've checked the situation. It's clear to proceed so next you will do what we call the ABC's of first aid. Does anyone know what the letters stand for?"

Someone calls out, 'airway' while another person calls out, 'breathing.'

"That's right. A is for airway, B is for breathing and C is for circulation. Zac is going to demonstrate how to check these so watch him while I talk.

Everyone's eyes zone in on Zac as Lily continues, "Starting with airway. You want the victim face up so if they are face down, gently roll them over." Zac turns the dummy face down so he can show us how to safely turn someone over. He places a hand on the back of the neck and his other hand on the hip, and rolls the dummy over. "Next you need to open the victim's airway. You can flick your finger in their mouth to clear out anything blocking it. Kneeling next to the victim, you place one hand on their forehead and gently tilt their head back, using two fingers on the chin not on the throat." All eyes are still on Zac.

"Now for breathing. With their airway open, you need to look, listen and feel for any signs of breathing. You place your ear by their mouth for five to ten seconds with your eyes directed at their chest to watch and see if it rises and falls. Also check for any signs of circulation, which includes groaning, coughing or any movement," she says. Zac leans back so we can continue listening to Lily.

"If the victim has signs of circulation but is not breathing, you want to move to rescue breathing. If the victim has no signs of breathing or circulation then that's when full CPR comes into play. I want you to split into groups and we are going to role play the first part. You will assess the scene, roll the victim over and then go through your ABC's. Once I'm confident you all have the basics sorted, we will move on to CPR."

We split off into groups and I join Rafe and JP, taking turns at playing the victim and the first responder. I can't help but giggle when Rafe tickles under my chin when trying to tilt my head.

When Lily and Zac are happy we have all learnt the first part, they move onto the CPR part. We stay in our groups but Zac moves back to the dummy in the middle of the room while Lily explains what he's doing.

"When you start CPR, remember the letters CAB. It stands for compressions, airway and breathing. Start with compressions. You are going to place one hand over the other and lock your fingers with your arms straight. You press down in between the victim's nipples. You want to push down about two inches so you do have to use a bit of force. For now, we will focus on what to do and then we will work on proper technique during our next lesson. You want to do thirty compressions and then follow with two rescue breaths. For the two breaths, make sure the head is tilted back, pinch the nose then blow two long full breaths into their mouth. Then start with compressions and continue this pattern until they either start breathing on their own or help arrives. Watch while Zac demonstrates again."

We all watch Zac as he shows us what to do. He does the compressions and I must say he uses a lot of force. I don't know if my small frame would make much of a difference in a life or death situation. Then he gives the two breaths and I focus on what he's doing. We finish up the lesson by practicing pretend compressions on each other.

JP and Rafe only want to do compressions on each other because Rafe says, "Petal, I'd feel uncomfortable if I copped a feel of your boobs." His comment has him and JP both blushing and me giggling. Their faces are so serious I couldn't help but laugh. After we've all had a turn, the bell rings signalling the end of class.

"Great work everyone. Next week we will carry on from there and take turns working on the dummy so you get the feel of real compressions and breaths. See you all then," Lily says, before everyone exits the class to go to our second period.

-- Tate --

Hanging up from Tamsyn was hard. I didn't want to go. I wanted to talk to her all day but I knew she would be late for school if I didn't mention the time. Listening to her softly snore for an hour before she woke up was the highlight of my morning. Being vulnerable and confiding in her how I'm feeling was hard. If I'm honest, my soul feels a million times better now having shared my secret with somebody. Can she help me through this dark time and pull me through the other side? I hope so.

I'm not in the mood for school but I force myself to get ready and face the music. I hope Avery got the message last night and will finally leave me alone. I text Xander to let him know I'm coming to school so he can pick me up. I make myself a coffee while I wait. For the first time in ages, I add milk and sugar and enjoy the taste as it hits my tongue. Living in a tasteless world hasn't helped me either. I need to push myself to persevere if I'm going to get through this.

As me and Xander ride to school, he mentions Pierce filling him in on the Avery stunt and how she had his phone.

"She's cray cray man," he says, and I nod because I completely agree with him. How else can you describe the way she has acted?

"What was school like yesterday?" I ask, dreading the answer.

"There were a few whispers about the photo but me and Pierce shut down any talk we overheard. At least now we know the full story and can tell people Avery set up the whole thing," he says.

"They're going to believe what they want anyway. People know me and they know her so if they believe her over me then I don't have time for them. I don't have the energy for this," I tell him, truthfully. I could care less what everyone at school thinks about me. My priorities have shifted since Quinn died. I guess it's times like this you realise who are the people most important to you and who you have time for.

"Preach it brother," Xan says, and I can't help but stare at him and smile. Him and Pierce have always got my back no matter what and I'm thankful for them, especially now.

"I know it'll be a sore subject but have you got plans for your birthday next Friday?" As his words flow through my brain, the colour must drain from my face because the next thing I know, Xander is pulling up in the school parking lot saying, "Sorry man, I shouldn't have brought it up."

"I forgot," I whisper, realising I hadn't been keeping track of days or dates so it had completely slipped my mind. Next week is going to be my eighteenth birthday. Not only mine but Quinn's too. She will be forever frozen at the age of seventeen while my life goes on and I grow older without her. The all too familiar pace of my breaths pick up and my wide eyes look to my friend for help.

"It's okay Tate. Calm down. You can control it man, it doesn't control you," he says, helping me to calm myself before the panic attack takes hold. "Let's just sit here a minute while you compose yourself yeah?" he says, and I nod. There's no way I can enter school in this state. I'd likely have a full blown panic attack before I left the car park.

I close my eyes, lean my head back and hear Xander talking but it's not to me. I peek out of one eye and see he's on his phone so I close my eyes again and wait. I know who he's called and he'll be here soon. A few minutes drag by and then Pierce is opening up the back door and getting in.

"You alright Tate?" Pierce asks, and I nod, not ready to open my eyes. I can contain it better if I keep my eyes shut and focus on keeping my breaths even. "Why don't we go get a feed? I don't mind missing the first period?" Pierce suggests, and Xander agrees.

"Sure guys, let's do that," I say, not ready to walk into school yet. Xander pulls the car back out of the car park and we drive to a McDonald's and go to the drive thru. Pierce mumbles out an order while I focus on pushing thoughts of my birthday to the side for now. I will have to deal with it later. We sit in their car park, munching on our food and the guys fill the silence with talk of a party this weekend, trying to distract me. I decline the offer. I'd much rather stay in than go out drinking again. No more parties in my foreseeable future if Avery is going to be attending. Not after what happened at the last party.

We stay in the car for a while longer and the guys even manage to get me to crack a smile. When we arrive back at school, it's already into the second period. We decide to wait it out until the bell goes, then we will go in and face the music. My thoughts can't help flit to Tamsyn and wonder what she's doing. I feel like her voice would calm me now.

"Guys I might go to the toilet before class. I'll see you guys at lunch," I tell them, and they both exchange glances but say their goodbyes as I leave. I walk around the side of the gym to use the toilets there. I relieve myself and then wait for the bell to go. That's my signal. I hurry to get my phone out of my pocket and dial who I need. I can't remember if she ever had her phone on at school or if it was always on silent? Something I never took notice of as I've never rung her during school hours. It only takes a few rings before her sweet voice fills my ears.

"Tate? Everything okay?" she asks, worried. I don't blame her. I only started ringing her last night and now I can't get enough. It's a complete turnaround.

"Yeah, I'm good. I needed to hear your voice," I tell her honestly.

"Did something happen?" she asks. I can still hear the worry there. I can see why she always told me not to worry when I would ask her if everything was okay. It's hard to open up and admit when you aren't okay.

I rest my head against the cold bathroom wall tiles, close my eyes and whisper, "I miss you." I tell her because it's another truth. Probably doesn't answer her question but it's the truth all the same.

"I miss you too," she says, and this time I can hear the smile evident in her voice.

We stay silent for a few more beats but I don't want to keep her from her next class so I say, "I better go otherwise I'll miss my next class." She lets out a sigh hopefully feeling the same. Neither one of us wanting to let the other go.

"Bye Tate," she whispers.

"Bye, Tamsyn," I return, as I hang up. Feeling better after hearing her voice, I finally head in the direction towards class. Right before I get there, my phone pings from my pocket, alerting me of a text. I quickly unlock my phone and see it's from Tamsyn. She's sent a picture. Desperate to view it, I click it open and it takes my breath away. She's taken a selfie, hair down surrounding her, with her tongue poking out and the sun shining brightly behind her. How is it possible she looks more amazing? My heart is racing but this time it's a good feeling. All because of this precious girl. How did I ever doubt she is exactly what I need to weather this storm?

Tucking my phone back into my pocket I walk to my next class. Knowing I have Tamsyn in my corner, gives me the strength I need to ignore all the whispers around school about me and Avery. When I catch my thoughts slipping throughout the day, I pull out my phone and glance at the perfect face of the girl who owns my heart. I've made the photo my new wallpaper on my phone. Her photo is all I need to make me forget about everything else.

Chapter 19

-- Tamsyn --

As soon as I heard his shaky voice, I knew something was wrong. He wouldn't tell me and I don't blame him. How many times did I tell him not to worry about what was going on with me? It's hard to open up to someone and confide in them when you're hurting. I'm still surprised he did last night. As soon as I heard him fall apart, all I wanted to do was hold him in my arms and comfort him.

The minute he hung up, I felt the loss of him. I keep wondering if this will be the last time I hear from him. Will he get triggered again and push me away? I wanted to think of something clever to send him like he did with his notes. I thought my smile might ignite one of his own. His warm smiles always managed to coax one out of me when I was feeling down.

So on the way to class, hair whipping around my face, I poked out my tongue and snapped it. I didn't feel great about my appearance this morning as I hadn't gotten much sleep but Tate never cared how I looked. He never made me feel less than. I could be wearing a garbage bag with vomit in my hair and he'd still make me feel like the most beautiful girl in the room. That was the only reason I didn't have any doubts when sending him the photo. I hope it made him smile and forget his troubles, if only for a split second.

I didn't hear from Tate for the rest of the day or the next. It's now Thursday afternoon and me and Penny are in our P.E gear, waiting to start our self-defence lesson. I haven't contacted Tate either, wanting to give him space. I'm planning on texting him after school to check in with him. Our self-defence class consists of only girls. I guess none of the guys in our year wanted to take it. Penny and I are partnered up and practising on each other. We repeat the same movements, over and over. Our instructor Tim said it's for muscle memory so if we are ever caught in a dangerous situation, our mind will magically remember and perform the moves without much thought.

Last week we practiced a lot of yelling and being vocally strong. Tim said we had to always be loud and make a scene, to draw attention to us, no matter what. It felt like we were girls gone wild, screaming and yelling at the top of our lungs at each other. It was a great release for all the emotions I had swirling around in me.

Today, Tim is teaching us about the importance of being alert and walking with confidence but not to make eye contact with anyone. He's gone through the critical strike zones; the eyes, nose, throat, solar plexus, knees and groin. JP's advice of kicking guys in the nuts makes sense now I know it's a critical zone to attack. We spend the rest of the lesson going through movements with our hands so we know which way to turn them to get out of holds, if we are ever grabbed. Before we end class, he tells us next week we will be working on getting out of situations where we get grabbed from behind. Leaving class, I feel more confident than I have in a while. I guess that's part of the lessons, to make us more confident in our own abilities to be able to protect ourselves, if the time calls for it.

Penny and I chat about our lesson as we walk out to the carpark. Me to meet the guys and Penny to get to her car. We've stayed in our

P.E. gear since it's the last period of the day. When we get closer to where JP parked, I can see the guys waiting for me by the car. Penny is parked a few cars over so she comes to say goodbye to the guys before she leaves. When the guys notice us, I see JP's eyes widen, looking right at Penny. I fail to keep the smile off my face as he doesn't take his eyes off her.

"Bye guys," Penny says.

They all say, "Bye," except JP.

He says, "Bye Pen," smiling at her. She shyly smiles back at him as she sways her hips on her way to her car. Once we are in the car, I give it to JP straight.

"When are you going to ask her out?" He turns in my direction, gobsmacked. He's shocked I've brought it up in front of the others. "Someone else might snap her up before you make up your mind," I say, as I smirk at him.

"Yeah I wouldn't mind a taste of Penny," Rafe blankly states, which causes JP to whip his head his way, punching him a bit too forcefully in the arm.

"Keep your mitts and any other body parts away from Penny bro," JP demands, and it has Rafe cracking up with laughter. Me and Scott can't help ourselves and join in.

"You're too easy to rark up dude," Rafe says, which has our fits of laughter continuing.

"Shut up," JP says, while he tries not to laugh at himself but he fails.

The guys drop me home and now in my room, I check my phone. Still nothing from Tate so I decide to send him a text.

Tamsyn: Hey, how was your day?

I want to send him another picture but I can't find anything around my room I want to send him a photo of. It's then I remember his notes in my drawer. They helped me so much when I needed it most. Maybe they can help Tate now. I quickly pull out the star picture; the one with the gap. Taking a quick snap, I send it with the caption, 'That's where you start letting the light in best friend.' Replaying his words back to him which he once used to comfort me. Instead of waiting for a reply, I have a shower and dig into my homework, to get it out of the way for the night.

-- Tate --

I've spent the last day and a half in a bit of a haze. The mention of my birthday has affected me in a way I didn't see coming. How am I supposed to celebrate my birthday when it's a big fat reminder Quinn isn't here to celebrate it with me. All I want for my birthday is to have Quinn with me but it's impossible. It doesn't stop me from dreaming and begging for her to come back in my head though. If people knew how many times I'd asked her to come back to me, they would think I'm crazy. Crazy for having conversations within my head no one else can hear, not even Quinn.

I didn't want to bring Tamsyn down with my melancholy so I chose not to reply to her. I was hoping I would be able to pull myself out of this funk myself. Here I sit though staring at her new photo, my hand shaking. She's sent my own star back to me, replaying my own words back to me too. I've managed to control my breathing this time. I thought I was letting the light in but the second Xander mentioned my birthday, I reverted back to my shut off self, not knowing how to deal with all the emotions I'm feeling. It's a war in my head. One voice telling me to call Tamsyn and share with her my messed up thoughts. The other voice telling me not to burden her with it because she doesn't want to hear it.

The need to hear Tamsyn's voice wins out in the end and I find myself in bed, early for once, dialling her number. She answers after one ring.

"Hey," she says. All she says is one word and it melts away all my worries. How this girl breaks and fixes me all at once, I'll never understand.

"Sorry I didn't reply yesterday, I was stuck in my head," I tell her honestly, as I snuggle down into my covers, getting comfortable.

I hear rustling on her end and then she says, "That's fine Tate. You don't need to explain yourself. I know how it is."

"Does it get any easier?" I ask, hoping she will know the meaning to my question without me having to spell it out.

"Hold on a minute," she says, and I hear more rustling before she comes back on the line.

"Sorry about that, I was finishing my homework when you called so I just put it away. Comfy in bed now, so I'm all yours." Her words increase my heart rate. If only she knew I already thought of her as mine, in every way possible. "To answer your question, I don't know if it gets easier, it's just different. When my dad first died, it felt all consuming, like I couldn't see a way out of it..." she pauses to let it sink in.

"That's how I feel, like there's no way out of this nightmare and I couldn't possibly face life without her. I don't want to be without her. Some days I don't know how I will survive without her," my shaky voice cracks. Confessing my hidden thoughts causes tears to spill and burn my eyes as they try to escape.

"I know Tate, that's how I felt before I met you. I was drowning in a sea no one understood because not many people in my life have lost anyone close to them like we have. They don't understand how some days it's a struggle to get out of bed or go to school. They see you laugh and so they think you must have finished grieving, right? But then you withdraw into yourself the next day and they don't understand. I don't think we will ever stop grieving for them. It doesn't go away but changes with time. Eventually it gets easier to breathe." Her words make sense but I still can't help feel I will be stuck feeling this weight on me for a while.

"I feel like I'm gonna be stuck like this forever," my honesty blurts at her again.

"That's how I felt before you helped pull me out of it Tate. I was going through the motions and coasting along, pretty much blocking my grief off because it was easier to not feel anything or deal with what I was feeling inside. It doesn't help you to live like that though, it's only hurting you. You've gotta go through the pain to get out of it."

"It's so hard to feel the pain of it all. I keep thinking it's a nightmare and one day I'm going to wake up and everything will be back to how it was. I don't know how to feel these huge amounts of pain without it taking control of me," I whisper to her, because if I say it quietly then maybe she won't hear me and I can pretend I didn't say it at all.

"Let me help you. I'll be here for you, however you need me. Just let me in please. Don't hold it in anymore and please don't push me away again," she pleads with me, and my heart splinters. I've put this girl through so much pain when she was already hurting and suffering through her own grief. I didn't mean to but I can tell I did.

"I'm so sorry I did that. I couldn't deal with the pain and if I'm honest, you make the pain come to the surface. It's as if my pain needs you to comfort it. It sounds silly," I confess.

"It's not silly at all. It's your heart's way of telling you to let your best friend be there for you. You need to decide if you are going to listen." I can hear the hint of a smile in her voice.

"My best friend is pretty smart," I say, letting the serious conversation go for now.

"Is she now?" I can picture Tamsyn's smile, as if she was sitting with me in the room.

"Yeah she's smart, funny and gorgeous," I admit, flirting with her.

"She sounds incredible."

"She is. But shush, I don't want everyone knowing how awesome she is or else they'll want her for themselves," I say, trying not to laugh.

"Don't worry, it'll be our little secret," she whispers before she giggles, and the sound has me closing my eyes, letting it soak into my soul.

"Damn, I miss your laugh," I blurt again. My mouth apparently has lost it's filter when it comes to this girl.

"I miss yours too," she says quietly, as if she's scared to admit it.

"I miss everything about you," I say with a sigh, my palms sweating from my confession.

"I'm right here Tate. I'm not going anywhere."

To turn the conversation away from seriousness again, I ask her about school and what's been happening. She fills me in on her life lessons and how her and Penny have become good friends. It makes me happy hearing she's found a good girl friend like her. We talk for hours, filling each other in on the day to day things we've missed while being apart. Once again, we fall asleep talking on the phone because neither one of us wanted to say goodbye or could bear the thought of hanging up.

Chapter 20

-- Tamsyn --

Tate and I fall asleep on the phone again, with him waking up before me. I'm starting to think he does it on purpose so he can listen to me snore. Although I don't think I snore. How would I know when I'm asleep, I can't hear myself. I should record myself then I'd know for sure. Gosh I hope it's not those big loud snores that thunder through the house and then have a whistle on the end. That would be so embarrassing.

I had to rush around again this morning to get out to meet the guys on time. This falling asleep on the phone is not good for my morning routine, it keeps making me late. But I can't complain because I love falling asleep to Tate's voice. I wish he still lived with JP so I could see him. Tate's forest green eyes flash into my mind and I hold the image of him there.

"Any plans for the weekend T?" Scott says beside me, pulling me out of my daydream.

"No, nothing planned at this stage. What about you guys?" I ask Scott and Rafe, while it's quiet in our human bio class.

"I'm hitting the gym in the morning and then meeting up with a girl I met at the mall last weekend," Rafe declares.

"A date?" I ask, shocked Rafe is going on a date.

"Petal, I don't date," he says, raising an eyebrow at me as he stares at me for a while, until my brain clicks. My nose wrinkles up in disgust.

"Eww Rafe, too much information," I say, and he barks out a cackle of laughter.

"You should see your face, Tamsyn. One day you won't feel that way about what I get up to," he chuckles at me.

"It's not the fact you're having sex Rafe, its the random sex. You're always with a different girl. Don't you wish you had a girlfriend?" I ask, curious. Rafe and Scott look at each other and have to contain their laughs so they aren't too loud and draw Ms. Chadwick's attention to us.

"It's not every teenage boy's dream to have a girlfriend. Some only want sex," Rafe states, and Scott nods along which has me wrinkling my nose at him.

"Are you all about sex too, Scott?" I ask. I didn't think Scott was like that at all.

"Oh no, I'm just agreeing with Rafe. If I had millions of girls wanting to have sex with me like Rafe does, I would find it hard to say no."

His confession has Rafe laughing so loud Ms. Chadwick's voice rings out, "Rafe, I'm glad you are finding the respiratory system so amusing but please focus on your work and leave the entertainment until after class." This has Rafe zipping his lips, locking it and throwing away the key at Ms. Chadwick. She can't resist his charm because she has the slightest smile tug at her lips before she returns her eyes to her laptop. Boys. I don't think I'll ever understand them.

When I get home after school, I hop straight in the shower and into my pajamas. I feel like zoning out in front of a movie for the night. I race down the stairs to get some snacks, so I can veg out and fill my mum in on my plans.

"Do you want any dinner or are you going to be full from all the junk?" she asks, as I struggle with my hoard of chips, lollies and biscuits.

"I think I'm good Mum," I say, turning my back on her to head up to my room.

"Okie dokie," I hear her say, as I disappear up the stairs. Dumping my goodies on my bed, I get the remote and start flicking through all the options on Netflix. Not sure what I'm in the mood for, I'm hoping my eye will catch something randomly to watch. I grab my phone out of my bed and get under the covers. Half paying attention to my scrolling, I unlock my phone to see a text. It's from Tate so I open it and I'm surprised it's a picture message. My breath catches as my heart gallops away. It's been so long since Tate has sent me a note on Friday. I didn't expect to ever get another one, but he remembered and sent one.

It's a photo of a butterfly and in the text he's written, **'This pretty creature happened to cross my path today so got a pic of it as pretty things always remind me of you.'**

My heart swells with emotion, my eyes burn with tears wanting to shed but I hold them in. I stare at the photo of the delicate purple and black butterfly until my phone rings and brings me out of my trance. Tate's name flashes across the screen.

I swipe to answer his call with a huge smile on my face and say, "Hey."

"Hi. Did you get my pic?" he asks.

"Yes I did. Thanks, it's beautiful."

"So is the girl I sent it to," he says, and I can hear the smile in his voice as my whole body flushes with heat. I'm glad he isn't here to see me. I don't think the colour of ripe tomatoes looks good on me.

I gather my composure and say, "Is that so?"

"It is," he replies and my own smile widens. "So best friend what are we up to tonight?"

-- Tate --

Talking to Tamsyn again has given me a new focus. Talking to her distracts me from my storm of grief. When I talk to her, I feel less darkness surrounding me. It makes me wonder if this is how it was supposed to always be but my dumb self pushed her away instead of giving her a chance to support me through this. I'm not going to make the same mistake again. I don't want to risk losing her a second time. I doubt my poor heart could recover.

The butterfly fluttered past me at school. While it sat on a bush by my class, I'd quickly captured it on my phone before it had flown away, saving it to send to Tamsyn. I've missed sending her notes on Fridays. Since Quinn died, it hadn't crossed my mind to do it but I hope she's missed them as much as I have. Those notes were our secret little connection, bringing us closer and reserved for our eyes only.

I'd been impatient all day wanting to send it to her but I'd always given them to her at the end of the school day on Friday. Plus I wanted to give her my full attention once I did send it. So I waited until I got home and was safely in my room before I messaged her. Once I sent it, I sat there with my foot tapping, waiting for her reply. When it had hit the five minute mark, I couldn't wait any longer and needed to hear her voice. She has become addictive again like the first time I saw her. She always pulls me in, without realising she does it or has control over me. I still find it hard to resist her magnet. I don't think I'm meant to.

"So best friend, what are we up to tonight?" I ask, after I've flirted a bit. I don't want to divulge all my feelings to her but I'm hoping she knows it, without me telling her how much she means to me.

"I was about to watch a movie, want to join me?" she suggests, and I crack up laughing.

"I'll get on my magic carpet and fly right over, shall I?" I say, wishing I possessed a magic carpet that could take me to her now.

"No silly. We can find a movie on Netflix and push play at the same time," she says.

"Have you done this before?" I ask, smirking.

"Nope, your best friend is smart, remember. I just thought of it," she says, laughing. I hope she never stops laughing. It's fast becoming my favourite sound in the world.

"Okay, it sounds perfect. I'll go shower quickly and get sorted. Give me ten minutes?" I ask.

"Cool, ring me when you're ready," she replies, so I hang up and race to the kitchen. I heat up some popcorn in the microwave while Mum gives me a funny look as I never do anything at speed lately.

"Going to watch some movies," I tell her without her asking, and she nods so I hurry to the shower. With my towel wrapped around my waist, I rush to grab my popcorn and a can of Pepsi. When I'm in my room, I call Tamsyn and put her on speaker so I can get changed.

"Look at you speedy, that was only eight minutes," she says, laughing.

"Were you keeping count?" I ask, while I open my drawers in search of boxer shorts.

"Honestly I thought you'd take longer than ten minutes, not less. Did you actually shower?" she questions with amusement.

"Yes I did. I'm getting changed now," I say. Tamsyn doesn't reply as I shut my drawer and drop my towel, pulling my boxers up.

"You who, you still there?" I tease.

"Yep still here," she says, her voice strained.

"You okay?" I ask, and she lets out a huff and I hear what sounds like a slap.

"Yeah," she drags out and I'm worried I said something wrong.

"You sure? You sound weird," I say.

"I don't wanna say," she says, her voice hitching at the end and it has me intrigued why she's acting shy all of a sudden.

"Best friends don't keep secrets," I say, holding in my laugh so she will tell me what is on her mind.

"Ugh fine, if you must know I was picturing you in a towel. Oh my gosh, I can't believe I said that out loud," she groans, and I let out the biggest laugh I have in a long time.

"I can't believe you said that out loud either," I say, between fits of laughter.

"Let's forget I said it, shall we?" she says, and I can hear her own laughter.

"You've got a dirty mind, best friend," I tease.

"Oh my gosh," she says, cracking up with laughter. "Okay back to the movies, what should we watch?" she asks, changing the subject.

"What have you got so far?" I ask, with the wide smile still plastered on my face. I hop into bed and get comfortable.

"I was trying to choose between Legally Blonde and The Sisterhood of the Travelling Pants before you crashed my party," she innocently says, not knowing what her words have caused. All too familiar now, my panic attack starts, short sharp breaths begin and I squeeze my eyes tight hoping that will stop it.

"Tate? What is it? Is it a panic attack?" I can hear the fear in her voice. Fear for me. As the images of blonde hair and green eyes flicker through my mind, I hear, "Just breathe, Tate. Don't think, remember. Don't think. I'm here. It's okay. You're okay. You're safe. Listen to my voice Tate. Focus on me." I listen to her voice as she distracts me, calming me down. Focussing on her voice, I'm able to control it this time. Tamsyn continues comforting me while I keep my breaths relaxed.

"Sorry, The Sisterhood of the Travelling Pants is Quinn's favourite movie, I mean was," I tell her, keeping my breaths steady.

"Oh Tate, I didn't know. I'm sorry," she says, but it's not her fault.

"You didn't know Sweetness. I'm okay now. Thanks for talking me down," I say, still focussing on my breaths to make sure it's under control.

"Anytime," she says, and I realise I let Sweetness slip out of my mouth. I've tried to avoid saying it, as I'm not sure I deserve to call her Sweetness after how I left her. I need to try harder not to let it slip again until I know we are completely alright.

"How about we watch something else?" I suggest, regaining my composure.

"Any suggestions?"

"Let me have a look and see," I say, grabbing the remote and flicking through the movies. Tamsyn had suggested girly movies so that's what I scroll through, hoping to find another one she might like.

"What about Chasing Liberty? I haven't seen it before," I suggest, my breathing back to normal levels now.

"Oooh yes, I love that movie. The actor who plays Ben is cute," she says, excited.

"Umm maybe we should pick something else if you are going to be ogling the actors," I say, laughing.

"Do I catch a hint of jealousy there?" she says teasing, before she laughs and I join in.

"Fine, lets watch it," I agree. I'd let her choose practically anything to watch if she got that excited about it. Hearing her happy, settles something inside me. A wave of calm relaxes me as we settle on the movie. We both snuggle down, get comfy and set up the movie, ready to start.

"You ready?" she asks.

"Count us down. Press play on start," I say.

"Okay, I'll go one, two, three then start. Let's go. One, two, three, start," and we both simultaneously press the start button. I ask her questions during the movie and she doesn't tell me to be quiet, she answers them. It's as if we are in the same room. That's how we stay for another two movies until our eyes get sleepy and we fall asleep on the phone again, which is quickly becoming our new normal.

Chapter 21

-- Tate --

Today is the day I've dreaded most of all. May ninth. The closer it's gotten, the snappier I've become. My heart and mind knew what was coming but I still tried to pretend it wasn't. It's my birthday. What would have been me and Quinn's eighteenth birthday to be exact. My dad asked me last weekend if I wanted to do anything for it and all I could give him was a blank stare before I walked away. Later that day I thought of something I wanted though and talked to him about it. He understood so said he'd make the appointment for me. I've continued to talk to Tamsyn during the week but didn't mention my birthday at all. If she knows it's coming up, she hasn't said anything. I don't even know when her birthday is. She's taken my mind off it. When I talk to her everything else vanishes into the background for a minute, until we hang up and it crashes back down on me.

It's a Friday and there is no way I'm going to school. I'll be lucky if I manage to get out of bed. I'm lying in bed like a zombie, staring at the ceiling when I hear a quiet knock on the door. I don't invite them in but I know they will come in anyway.

"Happy birthday," Mum and Dad say in unison, and they both come to sit on my bed next to me.

"Thanks," I reply, letting out a sigh.

"Are you going to school today?" Mum asks me, and I shake my head. I don't think I could face anyone. Not today of all days. Mum and Dad exchange looks between them, talking in that secret way they do.

Dad says, "Son, we know today is extremely hard because it's hard for me and your mother too." I hear him sniffle, so I flick my eyes his way and I see the unshed tears he's holding in, threatening to spill over. It causes my emotions to bubble up from where they were lying under the surface and tears fill my own eyes. He continues on after he wipes them away. "We know you probably don't feel like celebrating today but Quinn loved birthdays. Me and your mother thought we might go down to her grave and put some decorations and flowers down there." I can hear Mum's cries next to me so I offer my hand for her to hold. I've been so lost in my own grief, I forget they lost Quinn too. "We were wondering if you'd like to come with us?" Dad asks, and I stare at him and then my eyes glance to Mum, who's squeezing my hand tightly. They look so hopeful and I don't want to crush their feelings so I nod. Dad offers me a small smile and then says, "Why don't you get up, have breakfast and get ready then we can head down there?"

"Sure Dad," I say, returning his smile, trying to ease some of his pain. I lean over and give Mum a kiss on the cheek, which makes a light briefly return to her eyes. They stand from the bed and leave me to get ready.

I lean my head back and draw in three big breaths to center myself. Today is going to be a shit day no matter what but if I can lessen my parents pain, it will help me through. With a new focus, I wash up and change my clothes. The fact we are going to Quinn's grave has left me with not much of an appetite so I sip on a black coffee instead. Without caffeine, I don't think I'd have energy to do anything. It's what has kept me going for so long. Placing my empty cup in the sink, I turn around to find Mum and Dad at the kitchen table, waiting patiently for me.

"I need to do something quickly then we can go," I tell them. They nod and I wander down the hall to the back door. Sitting down in the yard, I find a bunch of the small flowers Quinn loved. I pick a couple handfuls worth and raise my gaze to the blue sky above. Is she up there watching over me? Can she feel how much I miss her? With a loud exhale I gather myself and walk back inside to my parents.

"Mum, have you got any red ribbon for these?" I ask, showing Mum the daisies I hold in my hands. She notices what I'm holding and her lips tilt upwards. We all knew how obsessed with daisies Quinn was.

"I'll have a look. Does it have to be red though?" she asks, curious why I asked for that particular colour.

"Yes, if you have it please," I say, remembering why Quinn chose the red door. I'm hoping the red ribbon will offer her some protection wherever she is now. It may not mean anything but I hope she can feel my small gesture.

Mum disappears into her room and comes back a few minutes later carrying a perfectly coloured red ribbon roll. She cuts two strips off the end and takes one handful of daisies at a time, tying a bow around each bunch.

Taking the bundles carefully back from her I say, "Okay, I'm ready to go now."

The three of us pile into the car and sit in silence. All of us, lost in our own thoughts on the drive to the cemetery. Once we arrive, we walk together to our destination. I hear rustling and I glance to where the noise is and see Dad is carrying a plastic bag, while I carefully carry my daisy bundles.

Our feet all stop walking at once as we look down at her grave.

"Happy birthday baby," I hear Mum sob. She can't contain her tears any longer and I let my own tears caress my face. I move to Mum's side and place my arm around her shoulders to offer her comfort. I need human contact. We stare at the white cross with Quinn's name across it. There's still no proper headstone yet but my parents tell me you wait to do that later on. It tugs on my heart and I feel as if this grief will never end. There will always be something bringing us back to the fact she's not here with us anymore.

I loosen my grip on Mum and bend down. With shaking hands, I place my two daisy bundles next to the white cross.

"Happy birthday, Quinny," I whisper, hoping she can hear me. I stay in my crouched position, staring at her name with thoughts rushing at me. The rustling from Dad's bag grabs my attention and then he's bent down next to me holding out a bright, colourful, plastic windmill. He holds out another to Mum and he keeps one for himself.

"I thought if we put these here, she might be able to feel us with her when the wind blows," he says quietly. I look at my dad, who has aged so much lately, and put my hand on his shoulder, giving him a squeeze.

"She would have loved them," I tell him, because it's the truth. She loved bright colourful things. She always wore the brightest colours. I can't remember a time where I ever saw her wear black. I push my one down into the dirt in front of the cross as Dad pushes his down on the left of it. Mum bends down and I help her push her one into the space on the right. There we stand, three little windmills all standing tall and blowing around Quinn.

We slowly stand and Dad rustles in his bag again, pulling out some plastic sunflowers.

He lays them down behind the cross and I hear him whisper, "So the sun is always with you. Happy birthday baby girl," before he comes to stand next to Mum taking her hand in his. Mum rests her head on his shoulder and we stand there silently again, lost in our own thoughts. I'm so absorbed by my thoughts when Dad touches my shoulder, I jolt from the contact. "Are you ready to go son?" he asks, and I nod.

I turn back to the small white cross one last time and whisper, "I love you Quinn," and let my feet follow after my parents, leading me away from her. The drive back to the house is as silent as it was on the way to the grave.

Once we enter the house, my dad says to my mum, "Honey, I've organised something for Tate today so he and I are going to head out for a bit." He leans forward giving her a kiss on her cheek. She looks between us but I follow my dad's lead and don't say anything.

"Have fun," she finally says, when she realises Dad isn't going to tell her where we are going.

Dad and I walk back to the car and once he pulls out of the driveway, he says, "I didn't tell your mother where we are going. I thought it might be better after the fact." For that I'm grateful, because I know Mum would try to stop me.

"Thanks Dad," I say sincerely, turning to face him.

He shifts his gaze quickly my way while maintaining his focus on the road and says, "It's okay son. I understand why you want to do it. It's a sweet gesture and I'm sure your mother will understand too. Plus it'll be too late by then," he says with a sad smile. It isn't long before he's pulling up in front of the tattoo and piercing parlour. "I've booked your appointment so all you have to do is tell them what you want and they'll take it from there."

We walk in and it isn't like what I thought it would be. It's bright and looks very hygienic. More like a doctor's office than a tattoo parlour. We are greeted by a guy with arms covered in tattoos who looks to be in his late twenties. My dad does the talking and explains he booked an appointment for me over the phone.

"I'm Dave. You must be Tate?" he says, staring at me and I

nod. I wonder how much my dad has said to him when he booked the appointment because he's looking at me with a sad expression on his face. He confirms my suspicions when he says, "So you want to get a tribute for your sister?" I let out a sigh and nod. My emotions I can usually contain are creeping to the surface, today of all days, and it's hard to keep them in. "And it's your birthday today? Have you got an ID on you?"

"Yeah, I do." I place my hand in my back pocket pulling out my wallet and showing him my ID. He's happy with what he sees and nods.

"Have you got an idea of what you'd like to get done?" he asks, and I fill him in on my idea. He listens, nodding along. "Where would you like it and how big are you thinking?"

"On the side of my ribs," I tell him, and I make a circle with my finger over my ribs to indicate the size.

He looks me in the eye and says, "That particular spot is going to hurt a lot." I already knew this as I'd looked it up on the internet but the pain doesn't bother me. Nothing can hurt me as bad as the pain I feel inside.

"It's going to hurt no matter where I get it right?" I say, and he nods, seeing the determined look on my face.

"Okay then, if you guys can give me about half an hour or so, I'll draw something up and then we can take it from there. I've had another appointment cancel so I've got time to get it all finished today," he tells us, which I'm happy about. It'll mean more to me if I can get it today, on our birthday.

"How about we go get some lunch?" my dad suggests. I nod and follow him down the street to the bakery, where we grab some sandwiches and donuts. We sit at the tables outside and eat quietly, not saying much at all. Once we finish, my dad goes back up and gets us a drink each. He hands me my fizzy drink and says, "Sip that while you are getting the tattoo. I've heard it helps to keep sugars up while you get it done."

I take the drink and say, "Thanks Dad. It means a lot you are letting me get this done."

"I wouldn't forgive myself if I let you go to some dodgy tattooist which you were likely to do if I said no. At least this way, I know it is getting done right," he tells me. "Plus Quinn would have been horrified if you got a messed up tattoo for her," he says, which pulls his lips up at the thought. I can't help but smile myself because he's right. She would have never let me live it down. She would have loved the fact I got one for her but she would have teased me relentlessly if it had turned out horrible.

We walk the few minutes back to the tattoo parlour and wait for Dave to finish up with his sketch. Once he's done, he pops around the side of the front desk, takes a seat opposite me and hands me his drawing. Looking at the picture in front of me has my hand shaking. It's better than I could have possibly imagined. My dad leans over to get a peek of it, his breath catches and he glances at my face. We stare at each other and as I see the tears in his eyes, I can feel my own eyes burning from the emotion I feel.

"It's perfect," I tell Dave, handing it back to him.

His bright smile shines at me as he says, "Great, shall we get started?" and I nod. He faces my dad and says, "It'll take a couple hours at least so you can come back if you like?"

"Okay Tate, I'll go find something to keep me occupied. I'll see you soon."

As Dad leaves, I follow Dave down to one of the rooms at the back of the shop and another tattooist comes up to the front desk to replace him there. He tells me to lie down and take my shirt off so he can prep my ribs. He does all he needs to and then places the sketch on my skin and has me stand to see if it's in the right place. I lift up my arm to get a better view in the mirror and it causes an excitement to pulse through me. I can't wait for it to be permanent.

Once we are both satisfied, he turns on the tattoo gun and it reminds me of the buzzing sound you hear at the dentist.

"You ready?" he asks and I nod. "Make sure you hold still," he tells me and I prepare myself for the pain about to hit me. The first touch is a burning scratch and I know the next few hours will hurt but I'm willing to endure the pain so I can have a piece of Quinn with me always.

Two and a half hours later and I'm gritting my teeth like I have been for the last half an hour, when the pain became unbearable. My only focus was on Quinn and to get it all finished today.

It isn't much longer when I hear Dave say, "Finished." I can't help but look down at it. "Have a look in the mirror," he tells me, so I hop off the table and stand in front of the floor length mirror, inspecting my new body. The tears I'd managed to keep at bay, come flooding back as I look at it. The two big angel wings run lengthwise, down the side of my torso. A dainty, red ribbon runs across them with her name etched on it. And to top it off, instead of a halo above the wings, I asked him to make a daisy crown, exactly like the one I placed in her grave. To me, it is the perfect birthday present.

"Thank you so much," I tell Dave, as I turn and hold out my hand to him with tears in my eyes.

"It was my pleasure," he says. He gets me to stand still so he can put some cream on and wrap it up so I can get home. He informs me of my after care and what I need to do, to take care of it.

I walk out of the room to the front and see my dad waiting on the couch for me, reading a magazine. I raise my arm so he can get a look at my new artwork, and a smile takes over his face.

"It looks great," he tells me, before his face drops and he says, "Let's hope your mother isn't too mad."

"Thanks Dad," I say again, meaning it. He nods and walks to the counter to pay for my birthday present while I put my t-shirt over my head. I slowly pull it over my torso so as not to hurt my already tender side.

"Okay son, let's go face your mother," he says. We walk out saying, 'thanks again,' and get in the car to go home and tell my mum what we've been up to.

As we enter the big red door, my dad grabs my elbow and whispers, "Let me do the talking." I nod because if Mum is going to be pissed off, it's better she yells at Dad than me. It is my birthday after all.

"Hi guys, how was your day?" Mum greets us, from the spot on the couch she currently sits in. I take her in and she looks so happy. I don't want to burst her bubble right now but it's like a band aid, better to rip it off and get it over with. Dad takes the seat next to her and takes her hand in his. Mum's brows furrow as she glances between me and Dad, not knowing what is going on.

"So dear, we have something to tell you," Dad starts with.

"Oooookay?" Mum draws out.

"I got Tate something for his birthday. It was the only thing he asked for. Now I hope you won't be too angry when you see it," he rushes out, and Mum looks at me with questioning eyes. Instead of saying anything, I pull my t-shirt carefully over my head, avoiding my ribs and turn sideways so she can get a better view of what we are talking about. She gasps, covering her mouth with her hand, closes her eyes and sits there breathing. I glance to Dad who lifts his hand in a sign for stop, meaning to give Mum a minute to compose herself. We both watch her draw three big deep breaths into her lungs before she opens her eyes, and I can see tears pooling in them.

"Let me get a closer look," she sadly says. My mum has never liked tattoos. I know this because her father would drill it into her any chance he got. In turn, she had drilled it into me and Quinn. Piercings she didn't mind but when it came to tattoos, she always said it was a no-go zone because they were permanent. I step closer to her and raise my arm so she can get a better view. It still has the covering on it so I carefully take it off, revealing the art work to her and the tears she was trying to hold back, rush forward and spill over in a downpour. "Aww Tate," she says, reaching out a finger to touch it but knows she can't because it's still fresh, so her finger traces the air instead. With a sadness in her eyes I wish she didn't have, she says, "Quinn would have loved it. I think it's perfect."

My jaw drops, eyes bulge and I say, "I thought for sure I was in for a lecture. Dad too, for taking me." She looks between us and leans back on the couch.

"It's done now, a lecture isn't going to change that. I know how hard today is so if this is the worst that comes from it, that's fine," she says, although she does turn to Dad and I see a glare of anger shoot his way. She will probably yell at him in private.

"Thanks Mum," I say, leaning down and giving her a kiss on the cheek. "I'm going to get cleaned up," I tell them, as I walk down to the bathroom to give them time alone. It was a good choice as I can hear Mum quietly berating Dad for taking me to get it. I chuckle to myself because I knew Mum wouldn't be able to stop herself yelling at one of us. I'm glad she chose Dad to yell at.

I close the door behind me and inspect my new tattoo in the mirror. I'm happy it turned out as great as it has. I smile to myself and catch it in the mirror. The expression looks so foreign on me. I don't remember the last time I saw my smiling reflection. I take a deep breath and release it, staring at the tattoo. For some reason it feels easier to breathe now. I think having Quinn permanently etched on my skin is the reason. Now she will always be with me no matter where I go.

"Happy birthday, Quinny," I whisper into the air, hoping she can hear me.

-- Tamsyn --

My week has gone fast. The life lesson classes are a lot of fun and make me look forward to going to school now. It could also have to do with the fact me and Tate talk on the phone most nights. If we aren't talking then we are usually texting while doing homework or something. He was a bit off this week, his mind is distracted but I'm not sure why. I was hoping he would confide in me but he hasn't yet. I'm sure he will in his own time.

I haven't seen JP since he dropped me at school but he had a furrow in his brow when he looked at me this morning. I have no idea what that is about either. It isn't until lunch, a few things make more sense. JP catches up to me in the line to get my food. We walk together to the door, leading outside to our bench. He tugs on my arm before I walk through it, stopping me.

"Tamsyn, can I talk to you for a minute?" he says, worried.

"Yeah sure, everything okay?" I ask, with raised brows.

"Have you been talking to Tate lately?" he asks. There goes the little furrow in his brow again. So it's Tate causing it.

"Yeah I have," I admit. I hadn't told the guys me and Tate were talking again but they must have noticed the change in me. I have been a lot happier lately, which is hard to hide.

"Did you know it was his birthday today?" he asks, and my heart slams into my throat.

"No I didn't." It explains why he's been a bit off all week.

"You understand this means it's Quinn's birthday too, right?" he quietly says.

"Shit." That hadn't quite clicked into place. My hands shake at the thought of Tate going through today. I was a mess on my dad's birthday. His birthday was the day Tate said he met me at the dock. The day I can't remember. To top it off, it's his own birthday and he has to go through this day without the person he probably wants there, more than anyone in the world. My own birthday is coming up soon and I'm not looking forward to spending it without my dad. It'll be the first one without him. "Have you talked to him today?" I ask JP, but he shakes his head.

"I texted him happy birthday this morning but he never replied." I can see the worry dripping off JP. He loves Tate like a brother so it must be hard for him to not be able to be there for him, especially today.

"I'll try to text him too," I say, and JP nods as we carry on outside to meet the others. The rest of my day is spent distracted by thoughts of Tate and wondering how he is. I didn't want to text him at school in case he replied so I waited until I got home, so I could be there for him if he needed me.

It's another Friday night I'm spending holed up in my room, with Netflix to keep me company. As soon as I'm settled under the covers, I dial him hoping he answers.

It rings and rings and just before I've given up hope, I hear his strained voice say, "Hey Tamsyn." He sounds tired.

I can't imagine the day he's had but I don't want to hide the fact I know so I softly say, "Happy birthday Tate." He doesn't answer at first but I can hear his laboured breathing through the line. I give him time, waiting, hoping he doesn't fall apart from my words.

It takes him a few minutes then he says, "Thanks," so quietly, I wouldn't have heard it if I wasn't eagerly waiting for a reply.

"It's probably a dumb question but how has your day been?" I ask, hoping he will be honest. I want all of this boy; the messy parts too.

"It's been hard. I miss her so damn much," his voice shakes, and I can hear the sniffles he tries to hide.

"I'm sorry Tate. I can't imagine what today's been like but I'm here if you want to talk." I hate that my words can't comfort him. No words were ever able to comfort me.

"Hold on for a minute. I'm going to send you something," he says, so I wait, not knowing what it could be. The notification comes through my phone so I put my phone on speaker and check the picture he's sent. My breath catches. He got a tattoo.

"It's beautiful Tate. I bet she would have loved the tribute to her," I tell him, not able to take my eyes off the picture. It doesn't help that the tattoo is on the skin of the sweet boy I miss. In my mind I can feel him, if I try hard enough.

"I hope so, because it hurt like hell," he says, laughing lightly but with the earlier signs of sadness still lingering.

"Can you explain the daisy chain halo?" I ask, hoping he will talk about her.

With a hint of a smile in his voice he says, "She would drag me outside when we were little and make me spend hours out there with her making daisy chains. I remember her always smiling and laughing in our yard, working so hard to get them perfect." He's lost in thought, remembering a happy moment with Quinn. "It's weird but having the tattoo on me makes me feel closer to her, like a part of her is still with me."

"I don't think it's weird at all. We all have our ways to cope and deal with grief, this is one of yours," I tell him. We are both silent for a minute then I break it by asking, "Have you got any plans for the rest of your birthday?"

"I was hoping we could watch some movies again. I'm all birth-dayed out, I just wanna forget for a minute." His words drift on but I understand. That's all I want to do sometimes too, forget about the fact my dad is gone. If I can help Tate with this small thing, then I will.

"Since it's your birthday I'll let you choose the movie but only this once," I tell him, hoping humour will distract him.

"You might regret that when I pick the scariest movie I can find," he laughs, and I cringe.

"No please don't do that because then I won't be able to go to the bathroom during the night. I'll be too scared," I say, hoping he will hear how much of a chicken I am right now.

It has him full on laughing then he says, "Fine then, no horror. Don't want you peeing the bed tonight." He starts cracking up again.

"Oh my gosh, that's so not funny," I defend, but then I'm cracking up and that's how we spend the rest of his birthday. Joking, watching movies, and distracting him from the fact he had his first birthday without his twin. Now I'm dreading my first birthday without my dad.

Chapter 22
~

-- Tate --

It's been a few days since my birthday. It was weird. I had moments where I forgot for a second it was my birthday and Quinn wasn't there. The moments I remembered she was gone were the worst; my heart physically hurt. I've started using my numb switch a lot less since I read the letter Quinn wrote to herself. I imagine she wrote it to me so I will push myself to deal with these feelings inside, instead of burying them in the dark. I still don't understand how Quinn could do what she did. If I dwell on it, it makes me angry so I shift my focus to the fact I know she wouldn't want me suffering. She wouldn't want me to go through what she did, so I need to persevere and let the light in.

Xander and Pierce came around on Saturday to hang out. They had messaged me on my birthday but I never replied. The same with JP. I didn't want to face anyone else that day. I almost didn't answer Tamsyn's call but my heart overrode my mind on that one. I'm glad it did because she took my mind off everything for a few hours.

My tattoo is starting to peel now, and it's bloody itchy as hell. I have to keep putting cream on it like the tattooist said. I believe having the tattoo has helped in a way. Xander and Pierce were as excited as I was to show them. Now they're talking about getting their own tattoos.

It's Tuesday today. I'm at school with the guys eating lunch. The rumours of me and Avery have finally died down. I think everyone was still wary of approaching me because of Quinn so no one has said anything. Avery has kept her distance too since I learnt the truth from her and I'm thankful. I don't need her drama in my life right now.

A vibration in my pocket distracts me from the guy's chat about Pierce scoring the winning point in his basketball game last night. I pull it out and there's a message from an unknown number. I open it and read the long message. My heart beat picks up pace but not because of a panic attack. This time they pick up because a plan forms in my mind. A plan I don't think I could stop if I wanted to because this time my mind tries to tell my heart what to do, but my heart kindly tells it to, 'Shut Up.'

I spend the rest of the day distracted in my thoughts. Racing through the big red door, I yell for my parents and put my plan in motion.

Chapter 23
~

-- Tamsyn --

It's been a few weeks now since Tate's birthday. We talk nearly every day. He sounded distracted again. I'm not sure why or what's caused it. I let him be, hoping he will talk to me when he wants to. I've had my own stuff on my mind too, which I haven't wanted to focus on. Focussing on school and Tate has been a good distraction.

It's finally the day for the observatory visit. They made us give up half of our Saturday to do it but the ones who did the fishing expedition had to give up their whole Saturday so at least it's only half. After being unsure about this trip to start with, I'm quite excited now. The self-defence classes have been fun and the sewing is coming in handy too, I must say. At least I don't need to safety pin my skirt now I've learnt how to take it in.

I get ready and then have a quick bite to eat for lunch. JP said he would pick me and the guys up about one o'clock. I'm rinsing my plate in the sink when my phone dings. I wipe my hands to dry them on the tea towel and open the message.

JP: Hey, outside. Ready when you are.

I don't need to take anything else so I shove my phone into my pocket. Since it's not a school day, we are allowed to wear whatever we want which is great. I think wearing our uniforms on a Saturday would have made this excursion way less fun.

"Bye Mum, I'm off now," I call to her, as I skip to the front door in high spirits. It's a sunny day outside with clear blue skies so should be the perfect day to see stars tonight.

"Bye dear, enjoy yourself," Mum replies from her seat on the couch, buried in a book she picked out from the library. It's nice to see her doing things she used to before Dad died. I get so caught up in my own grief sometimes I forget she lost her husband and it must be as hard, if not harder, as me losing my dad. We are both grieving for the same person but in totally different ways. I silently watch her for a second, taking her in before I open the door.

Closing the door behind me, a smile spreads across my face as I see Rafe hanging out the passenger window, waiting for me.

"Come on Petal, pick up the pace," he teases, with a huge grin plastered on his face.

"Yeah yeah, I'm coming," I say in reply, as I hop in my usual seat in the car. We drive to Scott's and he's already outside his house waiting for us.

"Are many students coming on this trip today?" JP asks, as Scott takes his seat with me at the back.

"Hey guys. Umm I think around twenty or so. I know a lot more wanted to do fishing when they heard they got to go on a yacht," Scott says, joining in the conversation.

"Why didn't you guys tell me it was a yacht? I could've worked on my tan," Rafe says from the front.

"That's all you would have done and we wouldn't have caught any fish. Plus Scott gets seasick, remember. We're supposed to be sticking by our mate," JP says, as he nudges Rafe with his arm to remind him why we all decided to go on this trip in the first place.

"Thanks guys, I appreciate it. Would've sucked to do this alone," Scott says.

"No worries bro, I'm sure this day is going to be epic," JP says excitedly, and I'm sure I catch a glimpse of him winking at Rafe. I have no idea what is going on with those two and to be honest, I don't think I want to know.

We pull into the school car park and JP parks up beside Penny's car. She sees us and waves as she gets out and comes around to my door. I scoot over so she can jump in next to me.

"Why did we decide to meet half an hour early? No one else is here yet," she whines.

"It's because you are always late, Pen. We had to make sure you arrived on time so you didn't miss it," JP says, with a smile in his voice from the front.

"I'm hungry. Anyone got any food?" Rafe asks, hopeful.

"You're always hungry," I tease him from my seat.

"I'm a growing boy Tamsyn, I gotta keep my muscles fueled," he says, as he flexes his bulging arms which makes me laugh.

"I've got a couple of muesli bars in my car if you want them?" Penny asks him.

"What flavour?" Rafe asks. "On second thought, it doesn't matter. I'll eat anything at this point," he says, rubbing his belly.

Penny opens her door and walks over to her car in search of the muesli bars for Rafe.

"How long ago did you last eat?" JP asks.

"Not long before you picked me up man, but you know me, I've gotta eat constantly to keep my metabolism going," he says.

"I think you use that as an excuse to eat whenever you want," I chime in, and he turns and winks at me, which has me smiling to myself.

Penny gets back in the car handing a couple of bars to Rafe. He doesn't check to see what flavour they are. He rips open the package and bites off half of the first bar straight away.

"Hmmm, it's hitting the spot," Rafe mumbles, between his bites with his mouth full.

As we sit there listening to Rafe chew his snack, other cars pull into the carpark. Blake's car is amongst them. Great, just my luck he had to be coming on the trip. It isn't until he gets out and is followed by Parker, Leyla and Chloe, my heart drops more. Looks like they are all going on the trip.

"Ugh, why are they coming to the observatory? They should have gone fishing and someone should have pushed them all overboard," Rafe says, and we all crack up laughing. It would have made my day if someone had pushed them into the water.

We catch sight of the teachers accompanying us on the trip, so we get out of the car and walk over to the big concrete stairs to wait for the bus. Ms. Chadwick is one of them, which makes me smile. She's always kind to me. It's a bit of a drive to get out to the observatory so I hope we can sit where we want. I don't want to be anywhere near Blake and the others. We don't need to wait long before the big yellow bus is pulling up beside us.

"Okay students, before we hop on the bus, Mr. Finnegan and I are going to be handing out name badges which are two different colours. The colour determines the group you will be in for the day. At the observatory, please stay in your groups until we get back on the bus.

If you can line up in an orderly fashion, we will hand your badges out as you get on the bus," Ms. Chadwick instructs us.

We all shuffle into line. Please let me be with Penny and the guys. If I get stuck with Blake and the others, it would be the worst day ever. As the line gets shorter, it's Penny's turn next. She gets handed her name badge and hops on the bus. Ms. Chadwick hands me my blue one, and winks at me as I take it. I follow Penny onto the bus. All the back seats are taken so we take seats at the front, where there's enough room for the guys to sit close by.

"What colour did you get?" I ask Penny, as soon as I sit down.

She turns her badge towards me, "Blue," she says, as I see the colour for myself and a grin takes over my face.

"Yay, at least me and you are together," I tell her, as we pin our badges on our tops. The guys all get onto the bus and one by one, they show me their blue badges. They take seats in the four seater space in front of us.

"Woohoo the blue crew. Observatory, here we come," Rafe hollers, and I can't help but feel excited knowing we are all in the same group. It will make this trip more enjoyable. The bus ride there doesn't take long at all because we chat and laugh the whole way.

Getting off the bus we are ushered to our two different groups. I see Blake, Parker and Chloe are all in the other group while Leyla is in ours. I don't let that get me down though, I will just avoid her.

As the bus pulls away to find a place to park, we all stand on the footpath, waiting to enter the observatory building. It's a brick building with what looks like a few different sections, all connected together. In the middle is the tallest structure which, from down here, looks like it has a look out point at the top. Off to the left there are two sections with dome structures on the top. I wonder why they are different.

"Now, you are to stay with your group at all times. Myself and Mrs.

Hopman will be with the blue group and Mr. Finnegan and Ms. Dawson will be with the red group. To start we are all together for a seminar and then we will split up. So follow me and enjoy your afternoon," Ms. Chadwick says, and then leads us towards the old brick building.

We follow her into the observatory and we are welcomed by a man in his late twenties, sporting a mullet. I didn't think mullets existed anymore. His enthusiastic smile takes over his whole face as he leads us into a lecture theatre. We all shuffle into rows, pull down our seats and settle in to listen. We aren't being graded on this so we don't need to take notes but we are supposed to listen. I'm seated between Penny and Rafe. I look around and can see Scott down the end of our row, pulling out a notepad and pen.

Our tour guide starts the seminar with information on the building itself. It was built before world war one and is a heritage site and public observatory. He continues on, saying they usually have either day tours or night tours. It won't be dark enough for the night tour since it's only the afternoon but they have an indoor night replica display we will get to experience, near the end of the tour. I lean back in my chair and focus on what he's saying.

Forty-five minutes later and he is done. He talked about the sun, moon and all the planets and then moved onto the stars and galaxies. As we are led out of the lecture room, we split off into our two groups. Our group is going to look at the sun telescope first. We traipse up some stairs and come out onto an open rooftop with a telescope there. As I look over the edge, I see this is the tall structure I saw earlier.

Our tour guide explains you should never directly look at the sun with your eyes or with a telescope without the right filters because it can cause serious harm to your eyes. With the telescope they have, it enables us to look at it safely.

"When most people think about observatories, they think about night and the stars but many forget about our closest star, the sun. The sun is a very complex object but is easy to observe. You can use different types of lenses to view different elements," our guide tells us. It's true what he's saying as I never considered we would be looking at the sun on this field trip. "Okay, so if you'd like to line up, we will take turns observing the sun through the telescope here. It is already fitted with the filters so there's no need to worry about your eyes," he instructs. We all move into line and wait our turn.

Rafe is up first and as soon as his eye hits the eyepiece we hear a big, "Wow," which makes me chuckle. It must be a good sight if it's holding Rafe's attention. As I'm watching Rafe, who is entranced by what he sees, I feel a tap on my shoulder which has me turning around. That's when I see it's Leyla.

"What?" I snap, as I fold my arms over my chest. She hasn't tried to talk to me since the day I blew up at all of them in the cafeteria.

"Can I talk to you for a minute please, Tam?" she asks with her head down, wringing her hands. I'm not sure I want to hear whatever it is she has to say but she looks nervous.

My head tells me we were friends for a long time and I should hear her out so I let out a sigh and say, "Yeah, fine." This has her eyes flashing up to meet mine and I'm shocked by the tears I see there, threatening to spill over. I wait for her to speak, not knowing what to say myself.

"I'm sorry about Blake, Tam. I didn't mean to hurt you, honestly," she says, as she begins to sniffle. "I liked him before you guys started going out and I was jealous when you two got together. I know it's no excuse for what I did but I truly regret it," she tells me.

"What made you suddenly go behind my back and start seeing him?" I ask her the question that has been plaguing me for a while. I never understood how one of my best friends could do that to me.

"After your dad died, we tried to be there for you Tam but you shut us out," she says, and it has me on the defensive.

"No, I didn't," I argue, trying to keep my voice down so we don't draw attention to our conversation.

She stares at me, sighing and continues, "You did Tam. You may not have noticed but you did. We tried for months. You stopped hanging out with us after school and on weekends. At school, you were there but it's like your mind was somewhere else. I know you were grieving for your dad and I should have been a better friend. I didn't know how to help you though," she says, and I listen trying to see through her eyes. She's right, I was spaced out. Nothing mattered after my dad died and I was barely holding on. I thought they'd deserted me but I had played my part and contributed to the mess our friendship turned into.

"That doesn't excuse you for going behind my back with my boyfriend," I tell her, because it doesn't excuse what she did.

"I know that. I was being selfish and like I said, I'd liked him for so long and when you were out of it, Blake and I started getting closer. It honestly started out as us trying to find ways to help you but then we got close ourselves. I didn't do it intentionally. It just happened. It doesn't matter now anyway. He was only using me. As soon as you dumped him, he dumped me. He never wanted to be with me," she says, hanging her head. She looks genuinely upset but with her it was always so hard to tell. I know what she was like behind other people's backs.

"So you two aren't together now?" I ask, though I think I already know the answer. She shakes her head.

"No. Like I said, as soon as you dumped him, he was pissed and dumped me too. He figured you heard about us from me. I guess you overheard me and Chloe in the toilets?" she asks, unsure.

"Yeah," I say, wrapping my arms around myself, holding myself together as I still don't like to remember that day. That's the day I completely fell apart.

"I'm sorry, Tam. Really I am. I didn't mean for you to find out like that. And I never meant to hurt you either," she says, as a tear finally escapes her eye and slides down her cheek. Rafe joins the end of the line then and gives me a concerned look over the back of Leyla's shoulder. I shake my head to tell him it's okay. "I was hurt too Tam," she says, as she wipes the tear away.

"Hurt how?" I am not sure what she means.

"I tried for months and I've been your best friend for years but you wouldn't open up to me. Then Tate comes along and I don't know, it's hard to explain. It's like the black cloud following you around wasn't there as often. Don't get me wrong, you were still out of it but I noticed you watching him, when you thought no one noticed. I was your best friend after all," she explains, and I stand there stunned. Did she notice more than I realised? All this time I thought she wasn't being a real friend. She takes a step closer to me and leans in and whispers so only I will hear. "That night at Penny's party, I came looking for you and I saw you go in the pool gate. I watched you for a bit. I know it was you and Tate on the pool chair that night." I draw a sharp breath in and move back, my eyes lock with hers. "I saw your face Tam. You looked happy which I hadn't seen in so long. And I knew it was him. He was the one who was reaching you, when none of us could and that hurt. It hurt, that as your best friend, I couldn't make you smile like he could. So I walked away and went back to the others, not telling them what I saw. I used that as an excuse to justify what I was doing with Blake," she says.

I stare at this girl, who for so long I considered my best friend, and realise she's right. I didn't let them in. I didn't let anyone in until Tate. I still don't understand why he got through when no one else could.

"I'm sorry too. I didn't realise I was hurting you by not letting you in. I wasn't letting anyone in," I say to Leyla. I think we both hurt each other and on my side I didn't realise I was doing it.

"I know it's probably too much to ask to be best friends again but I'd like it if you didn't hate me anymore," she asks with hope in her voice, and I nod. I can't deny her that at least. I think our relationship is too damaged at the moment to fix everything, while it's still so raw, but maybe down the track we could be friends again.

A smile spreads across her face as she says, "Thanks Tam." I turn to face the line again but hear her say, "And Tam, happy birthday for tomorrow." I look over my shoulder and give her a big smile of my own. She remembered.

"Thanks Leyla," I say, and then shuffle up to the telescope because it's my turn. I move to the eyepiece and look through. What I see is breathtaking. It's a spectacular orange colour. I think the last ten minutes have made this trip worthwhile.

After we have all looked through the telescope, we follow our guide to another room which he calls the museum. It is filled with displays, which we examine, as he talks to us about meteorites. As he talks, I see Scott busy scribbling notes down. He's the only one doing it and he asks questions as our guide talks. Rafe and JP are having a hushed conversation off to the side I can't hear. Those two have been acting extremely weird today. Penny comes up beside me, nudging me in the arm, distracting me from my thoughts.

"How cool was the sun?" she says, excited.

"I know right. It was so pretty," I tell her.

"I saw Leyla talking to you. Everything okay?" she asks.

"Yeah, we cleared the air. She apologised for the Blake thing," I tell her.

"You think you guys will be able to be friends like before?" she asks, and I hear the curiosity in her voice.

"I don't know. At the moment, probably not, because it's still quite raw but you never know what the future will hold," I tell her, feeling less weighed down than I have been. I guess I didn't realise how much it was weighing on me, until today. As our guide continues explaining the different displays, I glance over at JP and Rafe. They're both staring at me with cheeky grins on their faces. "Penny?" I ask to get her attention.

"Yeah?" she replies.

"Do Rafe and JP look like they're up to something?" I ask her, turning her focus to them.

"Why are they looking at you with creepy smiles?" she says, holding in her giggle.

"I don't know, they've been acting strange all day," I tell her.

"Beats me," she says, and her attention is back on the guide. I push the boys out of my mind and focus back on the guide, making the most out of what is left of this field trip.

Next we enter a room and the guide pushes a button, causing the ceiling to open up. The guide explains the dome ceiling is used to keep the telescopes free from damage from the elements. The room we are in rotates so we can observe all the different parts of the sky. The telescopes in here are used for the night tours mainly but we will get a chance to observe the sky, while it's still light out.

Lastly, we join back up with the other group for our final activity. This has the guide the most excited I've seen him all day. We are back in the lecture theatre where we started.

"Okay everyone, to start I want you to stand around the front here. Space yourselves out and take your time observing the projection and the different things you'll see. After a while, I'll instruct you to find a seat but to start we will stand." We all move away a good distance from each other. It's probably so we can observe without talking. The room turns dark and then the display starts, causing my breath to catch. It's beautiful. It's as if we are looking at a clear night sky without any pollution so you can see every tiny little star distinctly. There are millions of them. The room is quiet now as everyone absorbs what they are seeing. It makes my mind wander to Tate and the first note of the star he gave me. I know he would have enjoyed this trip as much as I have.

I peer into the darkened room and can make out the faces of the people closest to me. Their faces are all turned upwards in awe. I focus back on the beautiful display and get lost in it. I don't know how long we all stand there silently but out of nowhere, the hairs on the back of my neck stand up. A moment later my heart slams into my chest as I draw a sharp breath into my lungs and hold it. Someone has threaded their fingers through mine and their hand feels all too familiar. It isn't until he swipes his thumb back and forth across the back of my hand, I let myself believe it's true.

I let out the breath I'm holding as I say, "Tate?" turning towards the figure next to me. I see his perfect smile through the dark as his hand glides down the side of my temple and tucks my hair behind my ear. "You're here?" I ask, unbelieving.

"I couldn't miss my best friend's birthday now, could I?" he says, and the tears I didn't realise I was holding in, come spilling out. I leap into his arms, wrapping myself around him tightly, with him squeezing me just as hard. "Shhh, I'm here now. I'm here and I'm not leaving this time," he whispers into my ear. I pull my face away from his neck to look into his face and see his own tears, threatening to spill over. "I'm here," is all he says, and I nod, tucking myself back into his neck and finding comfort in the familiar earthy scent belonging only to Tate.

Chapter 24
~

-- Tate --

Approaching the observatory door, I spot Ms. Chadwick who is waiting for me. She catches sight of me and a genuine smile takes over her face.

"It's good to see you back Tate. I'm sure she will be happy to see you too," she says, winking at me. The day I got the text message from the unknown sender at school, a plan ignited in me and the more I thought about it, the more right it felt. It was Leyla of all people who had texted me, informing me Tamsyn's birthday was coming up. She said she wanted to make amends with Tamsyn and thought if she could persuade me to come back for Tamsyn's birthday then they could rekindle their friendship, if Tamsyn wanted to. I didn't want to come back for her birthday though, I wanted to come back for good.

It took a bit of convincing to get my parents to agree. They saw the determination on my face and I think they knew I couldn't be stopped. They flew down with me, not wanting me to come on my own and my mum wanted to see her sister again. I think they needed a break from home too. There are so many memories of Quinn in our house, it can be overwhelming at times.

I arrived here on Thursday and JP has been able to keep it a secret from Tamsyn. I'm impressed. He'd informed Rafe and Scott though and the three of them had been waiting for today as much as I had. My mum had organised with Ms. Chadwick to let me surprise Tamsyn here, because she wouldn't see it coming. What better way to surprise her than under the stars, which mean so much to the both of us.

Ms. Chadwick lets me quietly through the door and it's pitch black. I let my eyes adjust and slowly look down the aisle, searching for her. My sixth sense has returned and I can feel her near. It's like my soul can feel her whenever we are close. Goosebumps erupt up my arms when I spot her. Her head tilted upwards to the ceiling with a wide smile upon her face, makes my heart thunder. It's a good feeling, a nervous feeling. Gosh I've missed this girl. My feet have a mind of their own and as always, they lead me straight to her. I slowly step up behind her and inhale, my favourite smell fills my lungs. My body can't wait any longer so I step to the side and thread my fingers through hers. Electricity shoots through my fingers, racing up my arm at the touch. It's as if the connection has zapped life back into me.

I hear her hold her breath, so I run my thumb along my spot on her hand, back and forth so she knows it's me. Her wide eyes brimming with tears, turn my way.

The only thing I can think to say is, "I'm here. I'm here." I'm not sure whether that's directed at her or me but I feel my own tears form as she leaps into my arms. My body feels on fire from holding her in my arms for the first time in so long. My heart puts a piece of it's splintered self back together because of this girl, who I can't live without.

I don't know how long we stand in the dark, the stars illuminating the space around us, taking our fill of each other and letting ourselves enjoy this moment. Her head is squeezed into the crook of my neck, clinging to me tightly with her arms and legs. How I ever walked away from her, I will never know. I can only put it down to the fact my heart was so broken with Quinn's death, it didn't know what it was doing.

The guy who must be in charge of their tour tells everyone to take a seat. With Tamsyn securely in my arms, I wiggle into the closest seat, with her on my lap. I keep her there, not wanting to let her go just yet. The show eventually ends, lights flicker on and that's when my gorgeous girl raises her head. Tears have soaked her skin but the enormous smile plastered on her face tells me, this was the best decision I could have made.

"I can't believe you are here," she says, staring into my eyes.

"I know. It doesn't quite feel real, does it?" I say, as she shakes her head.

"Tate my man," I hear come from my side, as Rafe, Scott and JP come up. I hold out my fist for them to bump with equally big grins on their faces.

"You riding back on the bus with us?" JP asks, and I nod.

"Yeah, your mum dropped me off. She's organised it with Ms. Chadwick," I tell them. I see Penny come around the side of JP, giving me a small smile.

I know she's become part of the group so I say, "Hey Penny, good to see you," smiling at her and she returns it.

"Good to see you too," she replies, and I catch her eyes glancing at Tamsyn. Tamsyn smiles at Penny which has Penny's smile growing. They must be having a secret girl conversation. Does everyone know how to have these conversations with their eyes or am I just out of the loop? Ms. Chadwick tells everyone to gather around, telling us to make our way to the bus so we can go back to school.

The bus ride home, I have Tamsyn cuddled up at my side the whole time. We don't say much as the guys and Penny are there. Talk is mainly on the tour and how much fun they had. I'm content to just hold

Tamsyn again. When we get to school, I see Leyla looking our way with her own small smile on her face. I tip my head to her, acknowledging it was her who got me here and her smile brightens. She looks to Tamsyn but Tamsyn doesn't notice her. I hope they can become friends again one day as I know how much Leyla misses her.

When we get to the cars I'm about to pile in with the guys and Tamsyn but not before Rafe yells, "How about a sleepover Tamsyn, to welcome Tate back?"

His charming eyes stare into her and she says, "Sure. Penny, you're coming too right?" turning towards where Penny is by her car.

"Yeah, I'll follow you guys over. Have you got some pajamas I can wear?" she asks.

"Yeah, that's no problem. Cool, let's go," Tamsyn says. As we get into the car with Tamsyn in the middle, I pull her back into my side, not willing to let her go.

-- Tamsyn --

I can't believe Tate's here. I haven't let him go since he grabbed my hand. I'm scared that if I let him go, he will disappear. Now we are walking hand in hand to my front door. My mum is going to be so surprised he is back. Before I get to the door, Tate pulls my hand to slow my steps a bit.

It gives the others the opportunity to rush past us with Rafe yelling, "You snooze you lose, I'm going to get the best spot." They all rush into the house and Penny closes the door behind them, leaving us alone for the first time. Tate takes that as a cue to wrap his arms around me, bringing me closer to him so I squeeze him tight. Delivering a lingering kiss to my forehead, I let out a sigh as I feel peace run through me.

Pulling back to gaze into his eyes, I can't help myself as I reach up on tippy toes to press a kiss against his lips. He audibly sighs as he pulls me in tighter, deepening the kiss. All the feelings I've felt since we've been apart get unleashed and we cling to one another fiercely, losing ourselves in the kiss. Too soon and we are pulling apart, his eyes shimmering at me.

"Come on, let's get in there before they steal my bed," I say, chuckling causing Tate to join in. "It's good to see you smile Tate," I say, realising I have missed him smiling more than anything.

"It feels good too," he sadly whispers. I know how hard it is to enjoy things while you're still grieving so I don't say anything else.

Dragging him to my front door and opening it, I get blasted with party poppers going off, as everyone yells, "Happy birthday Tamsyn," and the tears rush to my eyes as I take everything in. There are balloons floating on the ceiling and coloured streamers decorating the living room. Off to the side, our usually empty dining table is now loaded with snack food, pizzas and a gigantic chocolate cake. Underneath the table, I spot bundles of presents.

"How?" is all I can say into the room, and they all laugh at my shock.

"Well bub, the guys here told me about Tate's plans to surprise you so I thought why not throw you a surprise party too," Mum says, with her own tears brimming in her eyes.

"You all knew?" I ask, still wondering how I didn't get a sniff of what they were up to.

"I only knew about the party, not about Tate," Penny defends. "But you guys nearly blew it giving Tam weird looks all day. Lucky I covered for you," she says, looking at JP and Rafe.

"I was just so excited for her to see Tate," Rafe says, with a big smile beaming on his face. I see JP and Scott nodding along in agreement with matching goofy grins on their faces.

"I'm gonna grab my bag from the car. Guys, you wanna grab yours too?" Penny says, and my mouth drops.

"You guys had sleepover bags packed already? What if I said no to the sleepover?" I demand, crossing my arms over my chest.

"That's why we had Rafe suggest it to you and use his charm," JP states, and they all laugh, with me joining in. The guys and Penny walk out, coming back a couple minutes later with their bags in tow, having hidden them in the car boot so I wouldn't see.

"Come on everyone, let's sing 'happy birthday,' then we can dig into the pizza while it's still hot," Mum says.

"How did you know when to order it?" I ask, still trying to piece everything together.

"Rafe texted me when you were heading back on the bus," Mum tells me, and I flick my eyes to Rafe who winks at me. They were all in on it. I'm amazed and blown away they did this all for me. "Come on everyone, gather round," Mum says, bringing us closer together and then they all sing, 'happy birthday,' to me off key. I can't help but think it's the best birthday surprise I've ever had.

We spend a good half an hour stuffing our faces with pizza, treats and cake before my stomach can't take any more. It's the most I've eaten in a long time.

"Time for presents I think bub," my mum announces, so they all gather around me as we sit on the couches. JP and Rafe move the presents out from where they are stashed. I don't want to think how they got them here without me knowing.

"Mine first," Rafe says, shoving a roughly wrapped present in front of me. He smiles excitedly at me so I rip into it and can't help but laugh.

"Press it's nose, that's the best part," he insists, so I oblige by pressing the stuffed pig's snout.

"I oink you," it says, and we all crack up laughing.

My eyes meet Rafe's and I say, "I oink you too," causing his smile to widen.

He leans over encasing me in his arms, whispering in my ear, "Happy birthday Petal," and delivers a kiss to my cheek.

I let go of him and move onto the next present which Scott puts in front of me. I don't wait, ripping into the paper. It's a binder with different coloured separators with a set of coloured pens.

I smile up at him and he says, "Now you can put all the notes I get for you in this, to keep them in order," while smiling at me. He leans over and gives me a hug. I can't help but laugh as my notes have been getting out of control lately.

"Ours are together," Penny says, gesturing to her and JP and I notice both their cheeks blush with pink. I open it in the same fashion I did the others. It's a set of green silk pajamas, a short sleeved button up top and pajama shorts to match, a couple of different shades of green nail polish and a green beanie. I love it all.

"Awww thanks guys," I gush, giving them both a hug. Tate walks over to the bags the guys carried in. Unzipping one, he pulls out two small, perfectly wrapped presents and walks back to me.

"Here you go," he says, placing them in my outstretched hands. I carefully unwrap one with shaking hands and inside is a pretty pink box. I flick the lid open and my breath catches.

"That's so you can take the stars with you, wherever you go. They are supposed to remind you to shine," he softly says, as I stare at the silver bracelet with the delicate stars, all hanging off the chain. My tear filled eyes find his and after a moment of staring at each other, he says, "Open the other one." Again, I carefully unwrap it. It's an identical box to the first. Flicking the lid off, I find a necklace and on the end is half a heart with the word 'best' inscribed on it. I look at Tate and he drags his own chain out, with his having the other half of the chain. Only difference is that his heart has the word 'friends' written on it.

I can't help but leap into his arms whispering, "It's perfect. Thank you." He squeezes me tightly before letting go.

"Best friends forever," he says, staring into my eyes.

My mum interrupts our moment by saying, "Okay bub, this is the last one." So I sit back down and she comes to sit next to me.

She takes my hand and says, "I know tomorrow is going to be hard since your dad isn't here," and the tears fill both our eyes as she continues. "Your dad was always adamant for your eighteenth birthday, he wanted to get you something. He kept going on about it so it's not only from me but from him as well. The gift was mainly his idea." She places a small box in my hands which isn't wrapped and I look at her with a raised brow. "Open it," she encourages me, so I do and it's a car key. My hand rushes to my mouth covering my shock.

"You got me a car?" I squeal, and start jumping up and down, unable to contain my excitement.

"Come on, it's in the garage. You will need lessons to drive it though," she insists, and our group is so excited for me we all rush out to the garage, following my mum. She presses the button, opening the garage door and there sits a cute little second hand light blue mini cooper. I instantly fall in love.

"Oh my gosh Mum, it's perfect," I yell in excitement.

"Your dad said it had to be second hand. When I first met your dad, he drove a blue mini so it took me a while but I managed to hunt this one down for you," she says, tears dripping down her face. I turn to her with my own tears, wrapping her in my arms and we stand like that for a few minutes. We take the moment to miss my dad and dwell on the fact he's not here for this. "He would've loved to see the look on your face right now honey," she says, wiping the tears off my face.

"Thanks Mum, I'll take good care of it," I promise. I spend the next hour looking inside at all the buttons and features with a permanent smile plastered on my face. I can't wait to drive it.

"Let's take it for a spin," Rafe suggests.

I look at him because I can't drive it so someone else will have to and then Tate reads my mind saying, "I can drive and you can sit in the passenger seat Tamsyn." He doesn't have to tell me twice. I beam at him and jump straight into the car.

"Penny and I will set up the room," JP says as he stands next to her, and I can't help but think he's using it as an excuse to spend time alone with her. Scott and Rafe jump in the back. It's a tight fit with three big guys but we make it work and they don't seem to mind. Tate takes my hand in his and that's how we drive. He doesn't let go at all. It's an automatic so he doesn't need his hand too much. I've never seen Tate drive before so it's an experience in itself, watching him in my car and I couldn't be happier.

We drive around the area for about half an hour before we head back home. Our happiness follows us back inside where we find Mum cleaning away all the pizza boxes and wrapping paper.

"Can we take all the treats up to her room, Tanya?" Rafe asks my mum.

She smiles at him saying, "Of course, go ahead, but if there's any mess, you are in charge of clean up duty."

She cracks up laughing when he says, "Aye aye, captain," saluting her. Scott helps Rafe juggle all the snacks up the stairs and they place them on my desk, creating a snack station. Rafe takes his command to not make a mess seriously. Penny and JP have managed to squeeze in another single mattress, this one an inflatable and I don't know where it's come from.

Scott must see my confused expression because he comments,

"We had to get another mattress to fit us all once we knew Tate was coming. Couldn't have one of the gang sleeping on the floor." I'm glad they've thought of everything.

"Penny, you wanna come get changed?" I ask her, and she fetches some pajamas out of her bag. I gather up my new green ones and we head to the bathroom together.

"You happy Tam?" she asks me, once we are locked in the bathroom.

"I couldn't be happier," I gush. I don't remember the last time I smiled this much. My face is starting to hurt from all the smiling if I'm being honest.

"It is so cute he came back for your birthday," she says, and I know she's talking about Tate.

"He said he's not leaving this time," I confide in her, and her eyes widen and her mouth hangs open.

"Oh my gosh, has he come back for good then?" she says.

I nod, saying, "I think that's what he meant."

She places both hands over her heart sighing saying, "That's so romantic." I can't help thinking the same thing if that is what he meant. I will have to confirm it with him. We slip into our pajamas.

"Wow these are so soft," I tell Penny, loving my new set.

"JP and I went shopping last weekend for it," she admits, blushing at her confession.

"Did anything happen?" I am curious.

"No, nothing yet but I feel like it might soon. For now, we are just hanging out as friends. Enjoying each other's company," and I nod, knowing what she means.

"Let's go back before they come looking for us," I suggest. Walking into the room, the guys have all changed. Rafe of course has no shirt on and neither does JP. I think that's for Penny's benefit. Scott, as always, keeps his shirt on and so does Tate which I admit I'm a bit disappointed at, but keep my face blank, not letting it show.

"Birthday girl can pick the movie," Rafe says, handing over the remote as he plops himself on the blow up mattress. Scott lies down on the mattress next to him and JP lies down on the one next to Scott.

There's one left but before I can say anything awkward, because both Tate and Penny usually sleep in the bed with me, JP jumps in and saves me by saying, "Pen, got your mattress right here." He pats the spare one next to him. She smiles at him and jumps under the covers next to him.

My mum walks in and says, "Okay guys, remember the rules. Keep the door open and don't have the T.V too loud. I'm off to bed." She leans over and gives me a kiss on the cheek as she leaves. That leaves me and Tate standing there staring at each other. Instead of being awkward, I hop into my bed and pull the covers back for him. He gazes down at me and I get rewarded with him taking off his shirt, and letting it drop on the floor. My eyes automatically zone in on his new tattoo. It looks more beautiful in real life.

He hops into the bed and I ask, "Can I have a look?" so he obliges, turning on his side and lifting his arm so I can get a better view. I trace it with my finger making goosebumps erupt all over his skin. A faint smile ghosts his lips.

"What movie are we watching Tamsyn?" Rafe yells from his spot, which draws me out of my haze, shaking my head. I flick through and click on the first action one I come across which happens to be Saving Private Ryan. The movie starts and I snuggle under the covers. Tate pulls me close to him so we are facing each other.

"I'm glad you're here," I confess.

"Me too. We have Leyla to thank," he says.

My brow scrunches as I ask, "Leyla?" I'm confused.

"Yeah, she texted me asking if I could come back for your birthday. She wants to be your friend again," he tells me.

"She talked to me today and apologised so maybe she does wanna be friends again," I say, as he tucks my hair behind my ear.

"Well that's a good start," he says.

"Are you back for good this time? You aren't leaving again?" I ask so quietly, I wonder if he will hear me.

He cups my cheek, stares into my eyes and says, "No. No matter what happens, I'm staying this time. If anything bad happens then we will weather the storm together. Always together." My heart fills with warmth and it spreads throughout my body. He pulls me into his bare chest, giving my forehead a kiss. "I'm sorry it took me so long to come back to you, but I'm not leaving okay?" he says, searching my eyes for any doubt.

"Okay," I whisper. His hand slides down my face as he pinches my chin between his thumb and finger. Gazing into my eyes, they flick to my lips for a moment and mine do the same, wondering if he's thinking the same thing as me. He pulls me closer, my eyes automatically close and then his soft lips are pressing against mine and my heart sews another piece back on. I wrap my arms around him tighter, hoping it will hold his lips to me as his tongue seeks entry.

We get lost in the moment but before we get too carried away, Tate pulls away, delivering a chaste kiss to the side of my mouth, and whispers, "Happy birthday Sweetness." I can't help the smile shining on my face. I stay wrapped in his warm embrace while we watch the movie and the two that follow. There are no more kisses but it still doesn't stop me from having the best sleep I've had in ages, wrapped in my best friend's arms.

Don't Panic. Keep Breathing.

Chapter 25
~

-- Tate --

We all spend Sunday, Tamsyn's actual birthday, in her room watching more movies. Everyone was happy to chill, spending the day lounging around with Tamsyn. I think we've distracted her from the fact her dad isn't here which is all I wanted to do. I'm glad I decided to come back and stay.

My parents are staying another few days to make sure I've settled back in alright. One of the conditions they have for me coming to live here again is that I need to see a therapist about my panic attacks and grief. Mum, with the help of aunty Sharon, is sorting it out for me. I know my parents are apprehensive about me staying here being as I'm their only child left but it's right for me. They have said they will come visit as much as they can. It was hard to leave behind Xander and Pierce again but once I sat down with them and explained about Tamsyn, they were happy for me and promised to keep in touch. They demanded updates on the green fairy front.

It's easy to fall back into my old routines here. JP and I pick up

Rafe on Monday morning, followed by Scott and Tamsyn. Seeing her again knits a part of my heart back in place I didn't think was possible. The darkness still plagues me but with her shining her light on me, I know I can face it head on instead of avoiding it and not dealing with it.

I have to go see Mrs. Davies again first thing but she says my schedule is the same as last term. All that has changed are the life lesson classes. She put me in first aid on Wednesday first period and car maintenance on Thursday afternoons. The sewing class she's put me in on Thursday morning has me raising my brows and asking why I got put in that class. She said it was one of the only free ones with spaces left. So I'm stuck with it. In English, they shuffle over to make room for me as Penny had taken my previous seat. I can't blame them but I won't lie, it did hurt a bit to see my spot taken. I'm happy to see my seat next to Tamsyn in human bio hasn't been filled, so I get to sit close to her and soak her in.

She lies down on her crossed arms in her all too familiar pose. Her head turns my way, a smile tugging at her lips. I notice her fingers wiggling under her arm and my own smile stretches across my face as I catch on to what she's after. I lie down on my own arms, scooting over and thread our fingers together. That's how we stay the rest of the lesson, clutching each other's hand, not wanting to lose contact.

It isn't until lunchtime Tamsyn tells me she's in sewing so I'm happy about being stuck in that class now. Every moment I get to spend with her is a reward. I'm also in her first aid class and the guys' car mainte-nance class so it has all worked out for the best. I'm lost in my thoughts, gazing at Tamsyn so I don't hear Penny's question.

"Tate?" she says, and I look at her with raised brows in question.

"Huh?" I say, my gaze flicking back to Tamsyn.

"I said we heard from a little birdy you've still got your V plates," Penny says, and I see Tamsyn's eyes widen as she stares at me, not knowing what to say. I feel my cheeks heat but it's only because now Tamsyn knows. I'm usually not one to get embarrassed about it. I glance at JP knowing he must be the little birdy but he has his lips pulled into his mouth, trying to hold in laughter.

My attention turns back to Penny as I answer, "Yeah I do. Any particular reason you're interested in my virgin status?" I'm not sure where this is leading.

"Oh I thought you'd like to know my girl here has still got her plates too," she says casually, as she takes a bite of her apple. My head whips to Tamsyn who is a dark shade of pink, all the way to her neck. She looks so cute, I lean over and give her a kiss to the temple.

"Nothing wrong with that. We are obviously both waiting for the right person," I say, directing my thoughts to Penny.

"How's the search going?" she asks, smirking at me.

I glance at Tamsyn out of the corner of my eye and then say, "I think my search is over." As the words leave my mouth, so does the water Tamsyn had sipped from her bottle. She turns a darker shade as I wink at her.

"Okay, give them a break," Rafe says, glancing at Tamsyn and holding in his laughter. He changes the subject and I can't help dropping my hand under the table, sliding it over Tamsyn's thigh and giving it a light squeeze. She gazes at me and we spend the rest of our lunch break, getting lost in each other's eyes.

The rest of the week goes by fast. My parents left on Wednesday night and it was hard to see them go. I feel lost again without them. I know this is where I want to be but if they were here too, it would make life a bit easier.

On Friday in human bio, I decide to write Tamsyn a note. It feels like a lifetime ago when I started this tradition and nothing will stop me from continuing it. She's much better than when I first met her but I know she still struggles. We haven't managed to spend a lot of time together alone but I'm hoping we can change that. I can't think of anything well thought out to write in my note so I decide to be honest. I rip a small piece of paper out of the back of my book and write, 'Your smile is amazing.' I slip it to her before the end of class because I want to see her reaction when she opens it. I place my hand with the note on her leg under the table, knowing her hand will meet mine soon. When it does, I slide the paper into her hand. She pulls it up to the desk, opening it and I get rewarded with the biggest smile as she glances at me. For a second I see the blonde hair and green eyes I miss dearly, but it's only a second and then it's Tamsyn in my view. I'm able to keep my breaths controlled by focussing on the beautiful girl in front of me. I draw in a big inhale, and along with it comes her scent, filling my lungs and settling me down. I'm hoping this is a good sign I'm not triggered too badly by her anymore.

That night we all gather at Tamsyn's again, for what's becoming our usual sleepover routine now. I get the bed with Tamsyn and the others, including Penny, are happy enough to lie on the mattresses on the floor. I notice wherever Penny is, JP is close by. I'll have to ask JP about Penny when the girls aren't around. I have some anxiety built up in me from seeing Quinn when looking at Tamsyn, but I've pushed it to the side and am trying not to think of it. I repeat the words in Quinn's letter over in my head, to help me focus on letting the light in.

I have another dreamless sleep that night, holding Tamsyn in my arms, and I can't help but think she is the reason. She puts my heart at ease now, helping me to relax. We all wake Saturday morning saying our goodbyes to her as we go. Her mum has got another girls day out planned with her and we don't want to delay them.

I don't have any plans myself so once we are back at JP's, I pull out Quinn's journal I brought with me from home. I feel the urge to be closer to her after seeing her yesterday, so skim through the pages reading quotes and thoughts that she had, getting lost in the pages as I do.

Chapter 26
~

-- Tamsyn --

My mum left to head out with some friends to see a movie. We had a full on girls' day. We got mani-pedis and massages and she still has the energy to go out and do something. It's pouring with rain outside and I'm exhausted, so I'm in bed with Netflix on. I'm about to drift off to sleep when my phone starts ringing. I grab it from the bedside table and a smile ignites on my face when I see the caller's name. I swipe across to answer it.

"Hey," I say, cheerily into the phone.

"I understand now," they reply.

"Understand what?" I'm confused.

"The dock. I understand now why you're always out here. It's quiet and so peaceful. Just like I wish everything was," he says.

"What are you talking about?" I ask, still confused because he isn't making any sense.

"I'm sick of being strong all the time. I can't do this anymore." He lets out an exhausted breath as he continues. "I just need some peace and I've realised how to achieve it. I'll be free soon; free from all this pain."

Tears start streaming down my face as he's scaring me. He can't mean what I think he does, does he?

"You're scaring me. You aren't going to do anything stupid, are you?" I ask, my hand trembling while holding the phone.

"I'm sorry. Please forgive me." He takes a big breath in before he says, "Bye, Tamsyn," and the line goes dead. I try to dial him back but his phone is off.

"Dammit." I race out of my room, not stopping to put shoes on. My mum still hasn't returned home so the only thought I have is to run. Run to the dock. Hopefully I make it in time.

My heavy feet pound on the pavement as I race against the clock, in the fierce rain, to get to him. I dial emergency services as I run, not knowing what I will encounter when I get there, but not willing to risk it.

"What's your emergency?" the operator says, as the line connects.

"Please hurry. Send someone to the old dock down on Basil Street. They were talking about wanting peace. I think they were going to do something stupid. I'm nearly there but please hurry," I ramble, between puffs from exerting myself.

"Who are you talking about Miss?" the operator asks, as I round the bend and the dock comes into view. Forgetting the operator, adrenaline surges through me and I close in on the distance to the dock quickly. I can't see him anywhere so I sprint to the end of the slippery dock where I catch sight of an empty bourbon bottle. Did he drink the whole bottle? Where is he? The light shining from the lamp shines down on the dark water below. I lean over the edge, eyes searching and searching, hoping I'll find what I'm looking for. It's hard to see with the rain pelting harshly down from above but I keep searching. That's when I catch sight of the familiar figure, face down in the water. Floating, unmoving. No, no, no.

My phone drops from my hand and on instinct, I leap into the water. No other thought in my mind but to get to him. I plunge into the freezing cold and as I surface, I gasp for air from the shock of the temperature. My arms splash through the icy water in a frenzy, in my effort to get to him. When I'm within reach, I stretch out my hand, grasping onto his wet shirt and pull myself closer. I struggle to turn him over as my feet don't touch the ground. I'm tiny next to him and I don't have the strength to turn his dead weight over. I manage to pull his head out of the water and twist it carefully sideways, so at least his nose is free to get air in.

"Come on, please be okay," I beg him. I use all the strength I can muster and swim backwards, dragging his body through the water to the shore. As my feet hit sand underneath the water, I gain some traction and it gives me enough strength to wrestle him over. With him face up and my feet on land, I continue to haul him up to the shore. Where my strength comes from, I don't know, but I manage to get him to safety.

I quickly check his pulse but I can't feel anything so I tilt his head back and check his airway. I tilt his head to the side and some water exits. I place my ear by his mouth but I can't detect any breaths so I start compressions on his chest, followed by two breaths into his mouth and repeat.

"Please, start breathing. Please, please, please. I need you," I beg, as the tears flow down my face. I look at his motionless face. How long can I keep up this CPR with him unresponsive? My emotions burst out of me and panic sets in that maybe I was too late to help him.

"Raafffeee," I scream at the unmoving boy, lying next to me.

I'm on the verge of giving up hope but my ears pick up the sirens, wailing in the distance. They must be close. I breathe another two quick breaths into his mouth and that's when he starts spitting up water. I help roll him to his side as he rejects all the fluid from his system. I cling to him, and move so I can place his head in my lap.

Wiping the hair back off his face, I whisper, "It's okay Rafe, I've got you. It's all okay now," repeating it over and over, as the sirens screech in the background. I'm not sure who I'm trying to comfort; him or me.

The paramedics arrive and everything becomes a blur as the adrenaline that helped me save him, wears off. Police are here too, talking to me but I'm not listening. My only focus is on the boy on the gurney, being wheeled to the ambulance. The boy with the brightest smile and the biggest heart. The first one to crack a joke to make you laugh. How did I not see it? While he was helping hold me together, he was falling apart inside. How did he hide his suffering so well? When did he become the biggest actor of us all?

To Be Continued....

Afterword

To my readers, I'm sorry. I know you are thinking, you can't do that. Not Rafe. It doesn't make any sense. After you read my explanation, hopefully you will understand why.

If my words sound wrong to anyone who has been in this type of position, let me first apologise. This is how I feel from my own experiences. I was scrolling through facebook when I got punched in the gut by a sudden blow at roughly eleven o'clock on a Monday morning in November 2019. That's how I found out my best guy mate had taken his life. Through facebook. It was an ordinary Monday morning. I was trying to get through having lost my dad in January and losing my sister at the end of September so I was already drowning in grief.

I went into shock. I tried calling him and calling him but it went unanswered. The more times I called and he didn't answer, the more my heart started to break. I saw more people commenting on the post. One comment confirmed he had committed suicide and I started to hyperventilate. My dog had to calm me down by jumping in my lap which he has never done before. I couldn't breathe, gasping for breaths through my tears as I literally felt my heart shatter.

His death has been the hardest to take because he took his life. He took himself away from me and that alone is a hard fact to come to terms with.

If you met him, you wouldn't have thought he would ever be the type to think about suicide. He had his demons as we all do to a degree. His demons however, were cleverly hidden behind big laughs and crazy jokes. He was the life of the party and would have done anything to ease someone else's pain in any way he could. I think he didn't want anyone hurting as much as he was. When my dad died, I didn't want to talk to anyone or see anyone and I declined all their offers. But Jonathon wouldn't take no for an answer. He rang until I answered and then he talked about random things with me sitting there quietly on the other end of the phone. When my sister died and it was the day of her funeral, I sat in the church before it started. It was Jonathon texting me crazy things to help unburden my heart of what I was about to face. I will always remember that because, for a minute, he made me forget and that was all he was trying to do. He wasn't there for me to turn to when faced with his own death which made his death even harder.

You are probably wondering why I'm telling you all this but it's simple. Suicide can strike when you least expect it. Sometimes you may catch the signs if you are lucky but then other times, there will be no signs at all. They say the biggest pain can hide behind bigger smiles. They would be correct.

If you are hiding behind a fake smile at the moment, please don't. Reach out to anyone. A family member, a friend, a teacher or a helpline. Reach out to someone. Don't hold it in. It's nothing to be ashamed about. Your feelings are never anything to be ashamed about.

Find something to live for. If it's the tiniest thing in the world, live for that when you can't live for yourself. Live for the next season of your favourite T.V. show, or your favourite concert. Live for the change of season if you have to. Simply find a lifeline and hang onto it with all you have. I promise you, your life may look hopeless right now but if you take life, day by day, you will feel differently. You will look back in two, five or ten years and think I would've missed out on so much if I'd gone through with it.

You may not think anyone will notice your death or it won't leave an impact but that's the darkness talking. Let me tell you; you are wrong. All the pain you feel at the moment gets shifted from you and passed on to those around you. If they don't know you well, you will still have an impact on them and that will send waves through their life they never saw coming.

If my friend was still here, I would beg him not to do it. Hell yes I'd be selfish and beg him to stay because I know how it feels to live without him. Without him, a part of me is missing that I can't get back. He stole the future memories we would have together from me. So I have to grieve for a life I thought he would be a part of.

Since I can't beg him, I'm begging you. Please don't do it. Please hang on. If you don't have anyone to help you fight out of the darkness, find someone or email me. I will listen. There is always hope. Some days you have to look harder than others but you can always manage to find a sliver of hope.

And to everyone else who has never suffered from mental illness or who has but isn't suicidal. Check on your friends. Check on the ones who cancel on plans, the ones who you see every day, the ones who laugh the loudest and are the happiest, the ones who have it all together and the ones who are struggling. Check in with everyone you care about, and do it often, because you never know when someone is fighting demons that are about to push them over the edge.

So I hope you understand why it had to be Rafe now. Without me realising it, he snuck into my heart and became my favourite character. Unlike my friend, I can rewrite Rafe's story and give him the happily ever after my friend sadly will never get. So just breathe, because Rafe will be okay. I promise.

Playlist for 'Don't Panic. Keep Breathing.'

1. Take Me Home by Jess Glynne
2. Grieving by Liz Bissonette
3. Tears In Heaven by Eric Clapton
4. Make Heaven Wait by Guy Sebastian
5. Someone You Loved by Amber Riley
6. Lay Me Down by Sam Smith
7. Rock Bottom by Caro
8. Never Be The Same by Jessica Mauboy
9. How Far Does The Dark Go? By Anya Marina
10. Why by Rascal Flatts
11. One Day by Tate McRae
12. One More Day by Diamond Rio
13. Rescue by Lauren Daigle
14. Smile by Nat King Cole
15. Fix you by Coldplay
16. I Won't Give Up by Jason Mraz
17. You Are The Reason by Calum Scott and Leona Lewis
18. In Case You Didn't Know by Brett Young
19. One Call Away by Charlie Puth
20. Holding You by Ginny Blackmore and Stan Walker

https://spoti.fi/33zra7E

Don't Panic. Keep Breathing.

Feedback

Did you enjoy this book? Would you like to give feedback? Did you know word of mouth is what makes the publishing world go round. If you enjoyed reading this book, please feel free to share your opinions or post a review online on Amazon, Goodreads or even on my Facebook page. We would love to hear from you. Or even better, let your facebook friends know and encourage them to read the book.

Check out my social on Facebook and Instagram or feel free to email me.

sarahdelany.com

@sarahdelanywrites

sarahdelanywrites@gmail.com

Don't Panic. Keep Breathing.

About the Author

'Don't Panic. Keep Breathing' is Sarah Delany's second novel and book two in the TNT Trilogy. It carries on straight after the events from book one "Don't think. Just breathe." She is one of eight siblings, has a loving partner and is a stay at home mother to their four young boys. Writing this novel was a therapeutic way for Sarah to deal with the pain and grief she suffered in 2019 after losing not only her father but also her sister and one of her best friends. She's a New Zealander who currently resides in Brisbane, Australia.

Don't Panic. Keep Breathing.

www.ingramcontent.com/pod-product-compliance
Lightning Source LLC
Chambersburg PA
CBHW020133120726
47903CB00007B/2242